S0-BIE-628

THE

MISSING MASTERPIECE

Attempted decision upon the Authenticity of the Masterpiece by Mr. Orlando Balchin, grocer and general salesman, Foreman of the Jury (a prominent Freemason)

THE MISSING MASTERPIECE

A NOVEL

By HILAIRE BELLOC
WITH FORTY-ONE DRAWINGS
By G. K. CHESTERTON

LONDON :: ARROWSMITH :: W.C. 1

First published in 1929

Printed in Great Britain by
J. W. Arrowsmith Ltd., 11 *Quay Street, Bristol*

LIST OF ILLUSTRATIONS

LIST OF ILLUSTRATIONS

LIST OF ILLUSTRATIONS

THE MISSING MASTERPIECE

CHAPTER I

A FEW years after the Great War, Mr. Henry Delgairn thought he would go over to Paris, and he asked his old friend, Sir John Pailey, the K.C., to go with him. He had not been to Paris for more than twenty years, but he had been taken with a sentimental longing to see the places where he had pretended to study art as a young man, and had vastly enjoyed himself.

Mr. Delgairn was the squire of a little village called North Merton, which lies just in that pocket where the counties of Sussex, Surrey and Hampshire meet, an easy walk from White's Selborne. His father had been a man neither poor nor rich for his rank, but on the richer side; he himself, under the new taxation and the conditions of the land, was neither rich nor poor, but on the poorer side. Neither of *his* sons could waste a year on an allowance in the Latin Quarter! Moreover, he was given to understand that the Latin Quarter existed no more. Nevertheless, Mr. Delgairn would go and visit its remains, and his friend Pailey, it being the vacation, must go with him, for Pailey had been his companion in those happy days.

The Squire of North Merton had been a widower

since the birth of the younger of his two sons, called Henry like himself, and now a boy eighteen years old at Harrow. The other son, John, older by two years, could not go to a Public School. He was a cripple, with a crooked back, a pale face, and far too sensitive eyes, whom his father pitied and loved, and yet could not help wishing he had been other than his heir. For the lad was not able to do the things required about the place, or to follow on his father's traces. He could not ride with any ease, nothing in the fields appealed to him, and Delgairn used to wonder what would happen to North Merton when he was gone. Harry was of another sort, doing famously, and well deserving of English land. But the heir, keeping apart from others of his age, well taught by a good tutor, yet (as he himself felt) doomed, seemed to have nothing in common with the place.

One great talent the poor young fellow had, and Delgairn would say sometimes a little bitterly that it was the one thing John had inherited from him. He understood how to draw and to paint—things which his father in youth had only desired to understand and had not achieved: he had enjoyed the life of the students too much to be industrious; and no man can master any art without industry.

Even young John Delgairn's one talent of the soul seemed to suffer from the same restrictions as had warped his body. He drew and painted nothing original; he showed no aptitude for the vision of beauty. What he could do was to *copy*, and that with a success so complete as to be startling and out of nature. The deformed are inspired by Providence to take to hobbies, and his father was glad enough to see the lad taking to this hobby of exact reproduction. It gave him an interest, it could do no one any harm, and it did not waste any of their now narrowed substance.

So Harry went on, in his school life, from one athletic triumph to another, and poor John pottered about at his singular amusement—one might almost call it his mania—for copying.

There were plenty of things about the house upon which to exercise it. North Merton was the regular old-fashioned squire's place, boasting half a dozen good pictures, a score of nondescripts, and any number of water-colours and drawings, engravings and little curiosities of all shapes and sizes, with no more than a domestic interest.

So things stood when their father decided to go off with his old friend to Paris to see whether the studio of the old happy days still stood.

They were only to be away a few days, during which Delgairn had an interval of leisure—for the harvest had been taken in on the home farm, and he had finished the first volume of the leisurely, laborious bird book he was writing; he only wanted a breath of change. He could be back in a week. Pailey was glad to go with him.

They found the place all right—though they could not find the Latin Quarter any more; it has gone up the hill to Montparnasse, and lost its soul half-way before it got there.

Paris is, so far, peculiar among the great capitals of Europe in this: that large sites which look as though they ought to be built over—for they are certainly valuable—remain waste; sometimes for years. Old gardens at the back of the Aristocratic Hotels on the Faubourg stand out against the pressure of the new things, and so do less protected empty spaces. In all this Paris still has traces of what London was thirty years ago. The tradition being good, it cannot last for long; but for the moment fragments of it do continue.

Delgairn found his studio. He went with Pailey through the rusty iron gates which both so well remembered—they did not seem any more battered than they had been before the Flood—he could have sworn that there was nothing changed in the ramshackle gravel path, and even the weeds and coarse grass seemed to have been there these thirty years—specially preserved to welcome him back. His spirits rose oddly. This gaunt desolation with the tall, grey, windowless walls about it, and the big studio at the back, its dirty wooden framework still standing, its ancient streaked roof of glass with a patch of zinc upon it, its rusty stove pipe coming out absurdly through a plastered hole in the brickwork, sang of the years when we were all twenty-one, and he welcomed it in his heart as he would never have welcomed a newer thing. As he stepped along that path he asked Pailey, almost in a whisper, whom they should find within? Manners might have changed, perhaps he had no right there? He must excuse himself as best he could; but he was hungry to get in under that north light again, and he knocked timidly at the rattling door.

A high, wild voice bade him enter. He saw before him something which made thirty years drop right off like a cloak. It was a man, very young, perhaps not more than twenty years of age, or a little less, with absurdly long hair, all shooting upwards on end, dressed in the holland smock of the trade, standing before an easel on which was a muddle—nothing describable—having on his left thumb a palette, and in his right hand a brush so big that you might think he was a painter of Walls rather than of Symbolist Art.

At the feet of this figure sat upon a little footstool a young dark girl, very hideous, very affectionate; and both met their visitors with a defiant gaze—they thought it was The Rent. For it was the Fatal Day beyond which the infamous landlord would wait no more.

I will now introduce you to something which perhaps you do not know. It is God's truth that there are such studios in Paris, or were a few years after the war, still to be had by God's starving artists for next to nothing a year, even there, with property worth millions all around: for such is Paris.

Why it is so I do not know: whether they have a system of leases even more absurd than ours, or whether the owners get more money by keeping a place derelict and letting buyers bid against each other for years—I say again, I do not know. One element of it was probably the after-war laws restricting rents to their late pre-war level in francs, although francs had lost four-fifths of their value. Anyhow, the poor old studio (call it rather a shed, and a dying shed at that) cost the genius with the wild hair and the too-big brush and the daubed smock-frock—him and his companion (who, I am ashamed to say, was called " La Mome Bouillotte ") the sum of sixteen English pounds a year, or two thousand of those brand new post-war francs.

It had been two thousand francs of the old pre-war francs, and that was eighty pounds a year—cheap enough, heaven knows: but the law had turned the eighty into sixteen—an insignificant sum to you, but a serious one for the wild genius with the too-long hair on his brush and the too-long hair on his head. And there was a quarter in arrears: and that quarter was five hundred francs, and five hundred francs is four great English pounds, and the genius had them not—nor he, nor La Mome Bouillotte. He had a rickety iron bed in a corner with a straw mattress, and three brown blankets upon it, and two cotton sheets. The bed had not been made, for it was only two o'clock in the afternoon. There was something stewing on the stove, from which the rusty pipe zigzagged up through the brickwork of the wall. The fire made the place much too hot on that summer day. There was one completely broken chair, and one not completely broken. There was the footstool on which the lady sat. There was a ruin of a Japanese matting upon the floor. Piled up in a corner there was a lay figure, a quantity of things that looked like canvases turned face to the wall in shame, two casks, a bottle and a broom—and in the midst stood the Servant of the Muses and of far-darting Apollo.

As he gazed at his two visitors, who bowed low with great courtesy, he was greatly relieved. They had not the manner of wicked men; they seemed not to be agents of Jewish landlords, wolves hungry for rent. But he was expecting such, he knew the respite would not be long, and he still half doubted.

Delgairn, in that reserved English way which the French admire as fantastic, but which to those who use it is second nature, told his reason for knocking—how, as a young man, he had himself used that place for his painting, and what a delight it was to him to see it again. How he would not detain his host a moment, only give one glance round for the sake of old memories.

But the young genius Bourrot warmed to such a greeting and bowed in his turn; and even the quaint and suspicious little monster on the footstool gave an awkward bob of the head as well.

In a moment they were friends. Bourrot had already, with a great sweep of his brush, begged them to look round (there was nothing to see), when there came another sharp rap at the door, not discreet this time, not with the traditions of the gentry behind it, but unmistakably the assault of that abominable monster the Bourgeois.

The Bourgeois has no heart and no soul. He lives upon the blood of the artist. He cannot tell the things of Heaven from the things of Earth—and he collects rent. The Bourgeois of all Bourgeois, the Bourgeois whom the old Latin Quarter vowed to damnation, ere the Communist came to the land to steal their thunder, the Bourgeois whom the new Montparnasse is sullen against, goes nowhere in more fearful guise than in the habit of a landlord, with bloodshot eyes and slavering teeth, gnashing and howling for his rent.

Yes, it was He indeed!

To Mr. Delgairn and Sir John Pailey, K.C. (and M.P.—I forgot that—O.B.E. too for ought I know) he appeared to be nothing more than a rather fat and dapper little Frenchman of about forty, in reach-me-down grey clothes. But to the Servant of the Muses and of Apollo, and to the Servant's Adorer, he was a Portent risen from Hell.

Then did Mr. Delgairn hear that conversation which recalled to him again his youth and his companions of youth, things which have been printed in a thousand books—the demand for arrears of rent from Genius who has it not: the protests: the insistence. He heard the Gallic irony, the Gallic scorn, the Gallic tenacity, the Gallic avarice, and the Gallic vision of things beyond this world, and the fixed Gallic determination to have the money there and then, having waited long enough, and no nonsense about it.

He heard—he could hardly believe his ears, so true was it to type—the old, old offer of payment in kind in lieu of cash, and the regal gesture towards the canvases against the wall, as who should say, "Take the lot! And be a millionaire in twenty years!"

Then the Englishman came back to the simple suffering of the thing, and did something natural to him. Bourrot, humiliated by such a treble meeting, and white with anger (while she whom I will call for the moment Madame Bourrot stood with clenched fists and angry tears ready to start) had turned to the shabby and much too thin coat which hung upon its nail (the winter clothes had been pawned long ago) and fumbled for what he could find; there might be half the amount, or a sop at any rate to stop the humiliation. While he was so turned, Delgairn paid the account, got the receipt, and the Wicked Bourgeois, to whom Delgairn had given that rent, had bowed stiffly to the two backs, to the coat, and to the two Englishmen whose fixed faces concealed so much heart and humour. The Wicked Bourgeois had shut the door behind him with a sufficient discretion, and was off to suck more blood, not indeed from a follower of the Muses this time, but from an elderly lady who kept far too much money in an iron box under her bed, and from whom it always took him twenty minutes of hard fighting to get his due.

The white and angry face of the Genius turned round;

the dark and angry face of the very short companion to Genius turned round at the same moment; they perceived that their enemy had departed. They did not at once understand what had happened, but when they grasped it, and when they had got over the second gust of another kind of anger, they had the simplicity to pass into a mood of extreme gratitude, and Bourrot discovered a phrase worthy of the ancestor on whose memory he doted, and who had said some excellent word or other on surrendering his sword at Leipzig. At any rate, what Bourrot said with quiet dignity was:

"Sir, I can only repay you with that which is not gold."

He gave Delgairn and his companion a rendezvous for the next day at the same hour, and said simply, as might the Creator on the Sixth Day, "You shall then see what I shall have made—and it shall be yours."

All that summer afternoon, inspired by those adoring eyes from the footstool, eyes about two feet above the floor, the grateful Servant of Apollo feverishly brought order and beauty out of nothingness, and under his much-too-large brush the Immortal Thing arose from the void into the world of lovely things—or at any rate, of things which it is impossible not to notice.

After the brief repose of a summer night, filled with great dreams of fortune satisfied and art triumphant, they rose, did those two lovers, washed the remains of the stew from the kettle, boiled coffee in it, cut off some stale bread, and the Creator dashed to create through the summer morning, while from the footstool the Adorer still adored He murmured strange phrases as the Thing grew, such as " For this I was born ! " and again, " It is the hour of my life ! " and again, as he furiously swung the bearded implement, " Never again shall I do work like this ! "

It rushed into being under his hands, and as it was evoked to immortality, Gratitude and Hate, hand in hand, were its Godparents.

" The gratitude," said Bourrot in a moment's pause, holding his brush like a sword as though to salute the woman who inspired him, " the gratitude shall be eternal, and worthy of this English lord : the hate shall be more eternal still."

Then he set furiously to work again, and La Mome treasured his words—which, she thought, should be as immortal as the canvas itself.

He stood back from it as the hour of the rendezvous approached. It was completed, and he saw that it was very good (or, as some would say, very bad). He said simply to his mate, " I will call it the Bourgeois Soul, and thus " (in rising voice that shook with anger and scorn) " perpetuate the crime in such a canvas as shall repay my benefactor a thousandfold."

The work was done. They sat rapt before it, he upon the chair that still kept together, she upon the footstool, and awaited the arrival of the to-be-dazzled recipient, the English lord—and his friend.

In size the Masterpiece (for by that name was it ever

Creative enthusiasm of a great artist inspired by gratitude

to be known) was in the latest fashion of the day, perhaps a foot across and eighteen inches long. He set upon it a chance frame, to bring out its values. In one corner was a sort of staring human eye; beneath this, criss-cross, a series of bands of a bright vermilion, but at an angle to these another series of bands emphatically yellow; and beneath them, as a field, a sort of mauve, very sinister; below all, upon the outer edge, was something which might have been a tropical fruit or a balloon but half inflated, and this was of a tender grey.

It was after a long adoration of the completed thing that Bourrot murmured, twice, "*L'Ame Bourgeoise*," and set his teeth in anger, though his eyes were radiant with pride.

"In effect," said the Adorer nodding deeply, "*l'Ame Bourgeoise*."

There came the expected knock at the door, and then the solemn presentation, not without conventional words on both sides, and profound and pleased obeisance from Delgairn, and even from the bewildered Sir John Pailey, K.C., M.P. and for all I know O.B.E.

"It shall dry," said the Master at the conclusion of these formalities. "It shall be varnished, it shall be brought by my own hands to your Hotel, it shall be yours."

In due time the Creator bore it with magnificence to his benefactor. He came back triumphant to the Adorer.

"It is bestowed!" he said.

She answered: "We shall never forget his name!" And then added, pensively, "What *is* his name?"

"I asked for his card," answered the Genius. "He had it not. It seems these Insulars carry no cards. But he told me that his name was de la Garne."

"But that one, that is a French name?" questioned the Adorer timidly.

"All ancient families in England have French names," her lover proudly replied. "He is a Lord. It is natural he would have a French name. His address I did not ask, lest I should seem importunate." Then he grew pensive and added, "It was my Masterpiece. Shall I equal it? Never! Do I grudge it? Not at all! By his good action he has enriched the world." And the Adorer heartily agreed.

* * * * * *

Thus was it that Mr. Delgairn found himself saddled with something which seemed to him very astonishing, but which he did not like to leave behind—it would have been a caddish thing to do. Besides which, it reminded him of a happy and amusing hour. Therefore it was that, a few days later, the Masterpiece, the *Bourgeois Soul*, was in North Merton House, trying to get hung; but in his heart Mr. Delgairn did not know what to do with it. He did not even know which way up to put it—it was in a plain white frame, with nothing on earth to show whether it ought to hang sideways or lengthways nor whether the famous Eye (which might be that of God's Justice or of Bourgeois Avarice, or a mere Eye, *pur et simple*) should menace from the top left-hand corner (if the picture were hung up lengthwise) or shoot glances upwards from the bottom left-hand corner (if the picture were hung sideways). He could not decide. He hung it lengthwise, and then for very shame slung it from a nail of a dark corner of the billiard-room, where a screen near the door cast a shadow over it and where it could disturb no one. There it awaited its day of glory.

CHAPTER II

OVER North Merton a year passed, as over the rest of the world. The unfortunate, crippled heir had had his coming of age, which had seemed to his father so hollow a festivity. The younger son was leaving school. John Delgairn kept more and more to himself and fell more and more as invalids and isolated souls will do, into the companionship of his hobby. He developed his amazing secret talent for reproduction.

That talent had been revealed to him by an accident. One day, when he had been making a sketch of the distant elm trees which he could see from his window on the edge of the park, he remembered Harding's pencilled studies of trees, and what a lot one could learn from them. Harding had taught his Father's Grandmother drawing in that very house a century ago, and if he looked through the portfolio he could doubtless find something to help him. He was not long in finding it, and with a close exactitude he faithfully reproduced the very touch of the Master, and there was the very mirror of it before him. He was astonished himself at the uncanny exactitude of the replica.

He thought it so exceptional that he got up to fetch an empty frame with which to try the experiment, whether each framed would give the same effect. Meanwhile he propped up Harding's original drawing against a pile of books, and his own side by side with it, like a pair of twins. He poked about among the frames in his cupboard in the next room. It took him some little time to find one that would fit. When he did, and as he came back to where he had been drawing and caught sight of the pencilled pieces of paper those few yards off awaiting him, it gave him a curious little shock to notice that, at such a distance, he was not sure which was Harding's and which was his own. It is true he was rather short-sighted, as are most very exact copyists. Still, it was startling. Of course, when he got closer he recognized at once which was which by the age of the paper; but the incident impressed him profoundly. He had found a congenial occupation for his lonely life. He would make replicas of this and of that, with the sole aim of exact reproduction. It was of no practical use in these days of photography and mechanism; it would lead to no reputation—but then, he desired none. All that he desired was something that would take him away from himself and fill his mind.

He deliberately chose the most diverse models, and as deliberately chose them without regard for beauty, or any other quality, save difficulty in creating an illusion of the original.

He began with an old faded water-colour of North Merton House as it had been two generations before; a small picture of no value except for its interest to the family. He took it from the wall of the schoolroom where it hung, propped it up, and studied his work. It was a full week's business, and it came to grip him so—he found his success so remarkable—that he could not leave it, but all day long, hour after hour, worked on at the strange task, interrupted only by two visits to London to get certain materials for the full result. The old water-colour was fox-marked; the plain gilt composition frame faded and slightly chipped, showing patches of dirty white. All that had to be identically reproduced; nothing else would serve him. And when he had made the last touch, he felt a kind of triumph. He had discovered an odd talent which he seemed to possess to the degree of genius. He remembered how Piazza years and years before, when he was a child, had come to reproduce certain MSS. for his father, and how, to show his skill, the famous engraver had taken two large cushions up from the sofa, hidden the original behind one and the copy behind the other, and then asked Mr. Delgairn to take them up and to tell him which was the original and which was the copy. It was like a conjuring trick, and he remembered how he had looked wide eyed on its success. Perhaps that was because he was only a child at the time, and now the test would fail.

It did not fail. No mortal could have told which was the original little picture that had hung on the schoolroom wall and which was the one proceeding from his own hand. He was so pleased that he thought he might for once attract his father's attention and interest to his work; but when he showed it him, he got no more sympathy than a conventional kindness. It was clear that he must keep his hobby to himself. It made him somewhat more remote than ever, in his father's eyes, from the part he would have to play when he came into the property.

When Harry came home for the holidays, his older brother told him nothing of the new interest he had. He was afraid of being laughed at, and, gentle as he was, he felt a little bitter envy of the gladness his father showed at the strong athletic young fellow who surely ought by rights to have had the inheritance of all that good land.

So young John Delgairn, with health continually failing, passed his time attempting all manner of reproduction, each specially chosen for the difficulty of the theme, until he recalled the Bourrot hanging in its dark corner of the billiard-room.

John knew nothing about the picture (for he troubled his father as little as possible in these last days). Even the name of the man who had painted it was only known to him by that one signature. But it was odd and absurd, and meant nothing, and would be therefore a greater test of skill. And after a very laborious effort he produced a result so perfect that it excelled anything he had previously attempted.

It occurred to him to force himself to a further test. He felt more ill than ever before. The more determined was he to prove to himself what he could do. The test he had proposed for his own satisfaction was this: he would make yet *another* exact replica of this monstrous absurdity. To add to the test he would make the second replica not from the first, but from the original. Then he would compare that second replica with the original, and see whether in the double process he had not lost some detail.

But no! In that very drastic test he succeeded as thoroughly as ever. He took the original Bourrot down again from its wall; propped it up in the full light by his window, with the two replicas on either side; and peering at them closely, and scanning every mark, smudge, and touch, not only on the painted surface, but on the back of the canvas, even down to the name of the man who had supplied that canvas, and even down to the used colour of the frame-wedges, even down to a tiny chip of wood missing from the back of the top of the frame—there was nothing whatever, to indicate which had come from the foreigner and which from his own hand: only the central position of the original, as he had arranged it. He took it up, went back, and hung it again on its place in the dark corner of the billiard-room where no one ever went; the two replicas he lovingly folded in thick wads of paper and put away.

His success had given him an odd feeling of completion, as of a whole life-task accomplished. And so it was; for he never drew again. The rest which he had post-poned too long could not set him right; and at the end of the summer, before the opening of the University term and Harry's going up to Magdalen, the sickly heir of North Merton was dead.

It is a cruel thing to say, but it is true, that Delgairn felt a half-conscious relief. When he looked at his remaining son, and thought how admirably he would fill the place which was now his by right, his whole mind was changed, and for the first time in twenty years the old squire felt content. In that content, four years later, when Harry was twenty-two, had taken his Schools, and was going down for the last time, Mr. Delgairn died.

As for the elder brother's poor toys and instruments, no one remembered them or cared for them, except one pensioned old lady who had been nurse to both the children and who alone mourned him at all. She had taken care to put the poor lad's things, his brushes and pencils, and his colours, and his two or three dozen sketches and parcels into an old oak chest, unlocked, which stood with sundry other derelict furniture and certain dusty and forgotten bundles of old papers, in the small lumber room under the roof which no one ever visited from one year's end to another. Then she in her turn died, when young Delgairn, for six years master of the place, was nearing twenty-eight.

The Masterpiece was ten years old.

CHAPTER III

Sir Henry Bensington was one of those men who make England what they are.

He had just that kind of strength of which we seem to possess the secret, and which is the despair of our jealous rivals. It was a strength which appeared in the rather heavy features, the well-poised head, and steady glance; but which was expressed much more thoroughly in the unfailing judgment. It was characteristic of such a man that, having undertaken one kind of business, he did not dissipate his energy by attempting anything outside that business. At the age of twenty-three—and he was now just over fifty—he had begun to deal in pictures. Nothing about him would have made you suspect the critic, still less the expert. Perhaps it was rather his strong will, determined energy, continuity of action, which had gradually taught him his own trade. But he had come in less than thirty years of labour to the very top of it, and was the chief man in England, and perhaps in the world, in his own department.

In discovery, in purchase, and in sale, even in manipulation, he was admittedly the master; and he had admittedly deserved and earned that very great fortune which none dared to estimate, but which ran

Sir Henry Bensington, from the picture by Sir Henry Offing in the Royal Academy of Sir Jasper Ottar's presidency. (This picture was bought by Sir Geoffrey Cowler, citizen of Pagston in West Riding, for presentation to Sir Hugo Buffle, Mayor of Pagston, reputed ancestral town of Sir Henry Bensington's ancestry)

into a larger seven figures than his greatest admirers would have guessed.

He had not risen from nothing. He had had the advantage of a certain capital to begin with, provided by his parents in Germany, and by an aged aunt in Milan ; and, what is invaluable to activities of his kind, a considerable experience of the continent of Europe. He had been born at Cologne, where his parents happened to be resident, and had received his early education in that town, which gave him from early youth the inestimable advantage of acquaintance with the German tongue. But he came over to London at the early age I have mentioned, and started the famous little shop which was the nucleus of the business in King Street. It was characteristic of the man that he should thus face the world single-handed and unsupported at a time of life when most of those who were to be his competitors were still wasting their opportunities in amusement.

From the first moment of his taking to the trade he showed, over and above exceptional powers of working and exceptional lucidity in the estimation of values, that he had one much rarer gift, a gift almost unique. This was a miraculous power of varying—quite suddenly—his aesthetic mood and appreciations. Nothing marks off the born dealer more sharply from the dull herd than this faculty. The many sink into a rut of affection and habit for such painters as they first knew. The exceptional brain which furnishes such purchasers with their needs can despise at a moment's notice what it formerly admired, admire what it despised, according as fashion changes or the making of a new market demands.

During the Fragonard boom, at the very beginning of his career, he felt Fragonard deeply. When Fragonard slumped, Henry Bensington felt, by a strange sympathy with the unseen forces about him, a lessening interest in Fragonard. During the much later Romney boom it was the same. But perhaps the most astonishing detail in this unique gift was his sudden wave of admiration for any great *modern* artist immediately upon death of same.

It was just when the public and the Press were fullest of the name that Henry Bensington was most inspired by it.

And all this was not owing to the effect of other men's minds upon his own : it was rather the other way. He had the mysterious powers of a forerunner. He would be found buying the work of half-forgotten dead masters, only singing their praises when he had acquired a considerable body of their work ; but then filling the papers and therefore the minds of the Élite with their glory. He was the better able to do this from a long-standing friendship with two of the few men who control our organs of opinion, Lord Borstal and Sir Charles Holloway. It would be difficult to say with which of the two he was the more intimate. And though they followed the high tradition of our national leaders in not allowing public rivalry to interfere with private friendship, their common affection for Henry Bensington certainly formed a bond between them, which was further strengthened by the fact that the more acute of the two splendid intellects (that of Sir Charles) had managed to acquire, under various names, fifty-one per cent. of the shares in Lord Borstal's principal journal.

For the first ten years of his business career Henry Bensington, though steadily accumulating, did not approach the very high position which he now occupies. There came to him a turning-point, as there does in the life of every genius.

Until that turning-point his reputation, though high, depended upon little more than the common talents for finding good work in unworthy hands, purchasing it with skill from those who could not estimate its value, and discovering the right purchaser among those who, whether on his recommendation or (more rarely) on their own choice, desired to buy.

He had also a growing reputation for his skill in procuring the exportation of Italian XVth Century and early XVIth century work, in spite of the law forbidding such export. But what made the great change in his fortunes, and put him on the summit where he has since stood, was the famous incident of the New York Customs, which stamped him at once for a man quite different from his kind.

It was a ruse worthy of a Napoleon or a Washington.

The Rembrandt which Meyer had discovered in

Budapest passed through his hands (only as agent—he had not then sufficient capital to advance for the purchase of it), on its way to cross the Atlantic to the collection of Mr. Fagdon, the President of the Mannawatta Corporation. While it was still in Henry Bensington's hands he caused the original signature to be painted over, and the name "Chas. Biggs" to be superimposed in clear and striking letters of a fresh vermilion. When this incongruous signature had thoroughly dried, he had it painted over again with the utmost skill (and behind locked doors) and from his photograph of the original signature had the famous "R" painted on again—and all this for reasons that will appear.

His next act was to advise in private fashion Mr. Carlos G. Pucker, the Hot-Dog King, what he had done, and to add to his letter certain recommendations, the reasons for which will also be apparent.

When the picture reached New York, and was in the hands of the Customs Authorities, they received an anonymous letter arriving by the same packet—and Bensington was its author. It warned them that the supposed Rembrandt was no Rembrandt at all. If they would assure themselves, let them not hesitate to scrape the signature, and they would find that it was a fraud, due to a well-known hack on the European side of the water, who turned out such things by the dozen—one Chas. Biggs. Those incorruptible officials took the risk; they scraped off the top signature; they discovered beneath it the fine bold red letters of Chas. Biggs's name. And all America had a good laugh.

When the picture reached Mr. Fagdon it was already almost worthless, and he sold it at a very heavy sacrifice to Mr. Carlos G. Pucker, the Hot-Dog King. That captain of industry had it scraped for the second time, and behold, on the departure of Chas. Biggs's name, the original Rembrandt signature appeared! The picture is the gem of Mr. Pucker's collection to this day. Mr. Fagdon cursed the bad judgment of Bensington as Agent, and Bensington apologised generously; but Mr. Pucker was the better client.

Mr. Pucker was really grateful, for it is rich men who best understand the value of money; he rewarded the European agent with new commissions, and by recommendation throughout all his world. Henry Bensington was made.

From that moment, as the saying goes, he never looked back.

He was knighted at the age of thirty-five—three years later—purchased the Longworth Collection after its owner's death by suicide. He advised continually for purchase to the National Gallery. In that capacity came a second notable action, far more subtle, which made such an impression upon his contemporaries.

He proved quietly but with insistence that the recently-acquired Gelée (whom our ignorant ancestors knew only as Claude Lorraine) was a fraud. He convinced not only the authorities, but the Press; and I must admit that the Press helped him nobly in his effort. It was unworthy of England that a spurious picture, however beautiful, should hang in the great National collection.

He did more. He approached those authorities, admitted that by his conscientious act he had gravely lowered the value of what had been thought a masterpiece, and himself generously stepped into the breach and paid for it no less than £250, although now that the fraud had been exposed it would not have fetched two hundred and fifty shillings. He went farther still in his almost Quixotic action. He begged that it might remain on the walls for some weeks, so that the public, which had been greatly interested in the controversy, should be able to satisfy their curiosity.

Strangely enough, in the course of these weeks an obscure friend of Sir Henry's, while protesting that he wished to do nothing disloyal to that great man, brought forward hitherto neglected proofs that the picture was genuine. They were proofs even more conclusive than those which Bensington himself had produced of its being spurious.

Bensington was not the man to stick to a wrong opinion from a false sense of honour. He frankly admitted that he had been wrong. The picture was a Claude after all (I mean, a Gelée), and he advised that it should be bought again for the Nation: a process that was the easier as it had not yet been taken from the walls. He himself, of course, refused to touch anything beyond the reimbursement of his original payment of £250. But he thought it only fair that the man who had triumphantly re-established the value of the picture should be offered a substantial sum. It was paid. (The amount was Five thousand pounds.) The obscure friend testified to his gratitude in no uncertain fashion, and the transaction was at an end.

The incident may seem a slight one, but it is characteristic of the man, and caused one of the Directors, himself well acquainted with the great business world, to remark that Henry Bensington would probably end in the House of Lords. A striking prophecy! For I understand, even as I read the proofs of this book, that he has been recommended for a peerage.

Such was the man to whose powerful mind that early Bourrot, the "*Ame Bourgeoise*," was to owe its perils, its high fame, its incredible career, its final refuge in the noblest of London's private collections.

CHAPTER IV

About two years before the death of Mr. Delgairn, the elder, and while Harry was still at Oxford, Sir Henry Bensington's unique and sensitive ear caught in the confused roar of the world the name "Bourrot."

There was good reason for his attention. The young man had got over the footlights with a picture which had had singular adventures, ending in a triumph. He had sent (he was himself ashamed of doing anything so conventional), but he *had* sent to the *Salon* of that year a picture of the purest symbolism, dealing with the mystery of man's fate after death. He had called the picture "*Le Néant*." It was a thing wholly new in the history of European art. Small (like all his pictures) less than two feet square, it was also, like all great things, superbly simple. It was an unrelieved black surface: nothing more: and framed in one of those narrow white frames in which this painter always presented his work.

The *Salon*, of course, rejected it. Inspiration of that calibre is rarely discovered: it rather imposes itself. Not only was it rejected by the Hanging Committee of the *Salon*, but also by the *Independent*, the *Nouvel Independent*, the *Décadant*, and even the *Eccentrique*.

Genuine adoration of The Slav Prophet (accompanied by the Duchess and the Academician) for the Symbolic Representation of the After-life

At last, with difficulty, Bourrot managed to get it shown at the *Absolu.*

There was in Paris, happily for the reputation of Art, one man with sufficient Vision. This was the small, delicate critic with the sensitive voice whom Mont Parnasse called The Slav Prophet, and indeed it was his custom to sign over the *nom de plume* of CRSK, until his editor persuaded him with difficulty to add a vowel, and expand it to CRESK. That signature ruled taste. His mastery over all instructed opinion was the more remarkable when one considers his origins, and that his parents, still happily surviving, were healthy, well-to-do peasants of the Champagne—much prouder of their son's fame in the capital than he was of them.

This mysterious figure was naturally in hot demand among the great; but CRESK was as daintily selective in his choice of friends as he was in his judgment of canvases. In a host of worldly acquaintance, there were but two whom he could call friends. One was the Duchess of Creil, and the other the elderly and distinguished Charles de Mallencourt, Academician. These were his only two real intimates among the great, but through them he ruled the picture market of Paris.

When "*Le Néant*" first burst upon his eyes he was alone. Indeed, he had only strolled into the *Absolu* to escape a violent thunderstorm. He did not affect these unfashionable exhibitions. But "*Le Néant*" struck him like a blow. He went out from the place in a dream, and in the nearest café wrote and wrote and wrote. Next day the article appeared in the newspaper *Petrone*, and a name which none had hitherto heard rose enormously like a meteor, and remained shining above the city—the name of Bourrot.

Cresk himself would stand worshipping it by the hour, bringing to the shrine those whom he ruled and who in their turn rule the clique which makes the market. And, with the closing of the *Absolu*, "*Le Néant*" was bought for the Nation by M. Machabée, whose wife was a close friend of M. Bernard, the Minister for Fine Arts. It went to the Luxembourg.

If there are artists whom too sudden success spoils, Bourrot was not one of them. With the next year he surpassed the glories of "*Le Néant*" in the still greater triumph of his "*Amour Perdu*," the profound meaning of which struck straight to the modern soul.

M. Machabée's brother, Charles Grant McCabe of Chicago, bought it for five thousand dollars, and toured the States with it under the title of "*Ah me, the Years!*" having it explained in every township of the Middle West by an expert Gaul hired for the purpose at ten dollars a spout. This oracle translated its emotional appeal to such of the populace as might not plumb the depths of contemporary art.

So for twelve months Sir Henry Bensington had been watching this new star, when there came a telephone message from his Observer beyond the Atlantic, which informed him that the moment had come to act. Carlos

Enthusiasm of the public of the Great Republic for the symbolic representation of Love destroyed by the Years

Pucker had bought the "*Amour Perdu*," and had paid twenty-five thousand dollars for it.

There was no time to lose. The telephone message had been spoken at New York a little after ten in the morning, within a few minutes of its sender's getting the news. That was just after three, London time. Before four o'clock every arrangement had been made and Henry Bensington was flying south to Paris in good clear weather and calm, some two thousand feet above the coast of Kent. Before dinner he had rung up the Bourrot household, and at cocktail he was in the flat.

Bourrot was *dans ses meubles* (excuse me! I mean "set up in style"). His poverty had departed, but not his simplicity. Still less his Adorer. He knew that he was famous; the sums he had already received, £500 for his first picture, £1,000 for the second, still dazzled him. When he heard the name and the voice of Henry Bensington upon the telephone he was as moved as though the great dealer had come to see him twenty months before, when no one had heard his name, and he received the Master of All Picture Buying like a royalty. Nor was he disappointed.

Bensington had grasped in the first five minutes the main points of the situation. Bourrot, he could see at a glance, was a dying man; and he could see in the woman's face that she knew it.

Bourrot with the candour of a creator talked as openly as a child. Yes, he had not a few canvases by him.

He would show them to Sir Henry. He was choosing the subject for his next to send it in in a few weeks' time, but he had not done much of late ; he was feeling oddly ill and not up to things. He would get better. Meanwhile how he wished that he could show Sir Henry what he knew to be his Masterpiece ! And the Adorer said :

" Ah, yes ! Sir Henry, he was young ! " and she cast up her eyes.

Then the story of the Masterpiece was told, and Bourrot shook his head as he recalled it. And the Adorer sighed.

" Yet it was not lost after all," he added, his fevered eyes shining. " It was an act of homage, and that is never lost. Nevertheless, if only I could find it—if only I could hear of it ! "

Sir Henry was pressed to stay and eat a meal with them. He did so gladly, and heard with further emphasis of the Masterpiece. Of how it was called " *L'Ame Bourgeoise* " and why. Of the occasion on which the English lord had done so generous a deed : of his name, de la Garne. Bensington's mind inwardly snapped upon that inexistent title, but his face showed nothing. He only nodded familiarly, as though he knew all about it.

" Could you find out, do you think ? " said Bourrot anxiously. " Not that it must leave the generous hands which hold it, but that I may see it again, or at least know where it is ? "

Bensington again nodded carelessly, as though the

matter was a sure thing, and then turned to another subject, of interest to both. He had come as a buyer. He made, as was his wont, without loss of time and very simply, the proposition which raised the Bourrot *ménage* to the heavens. He would willingly buy all Bourrot's work which he had been shown and all his future work, at £1,200 the canvas ; and Bourrot should limit the contract to a certain fixed number of years if he liked—say ten years ; or would he like it even shorter ? But Bensington knew well that there was not ten years' life in that face, nor even ten months.

This, said quietly over the coffee, was something more than fame. It was a great deal of immediate capital. And the fevered eyes grew brighter still, and the hostess smiled an ecstatic smile.

Sir Henry perceived that they would have taken less ; but according to the calculation which he was rapidly making he was secure enough. He had never been niggling, he had always flown straight for the big game. There were not half a dozen pieces to be acquired. There might perhaps be one more before the end : at the most two. And the prices *after* death would soar to anything you like.

So was the bargain concluded, and three human beings in their various ways were very happy over the coffee that night. Bensington, as he rose to go early, had become a firm friend, and as he took his hat in the hall he turned to his host and hostess, who had accompanied him to the door, and said :

"Oh, by the way" (his colloquial French was good)—"I have got to find that early one of yours—the one you call the Masterpiece, the '*Ame Bourgeoise*,'—haven't I?"

They both answered eagerly, "Yes, oh yes!" and the Adorer clasped her hands.

"Well," said Bensington, turning back towards the room, "look here; wouldn't it be just as well if you were to write me a short note, and what you remember of the name, and I will do my best. Anything will do—something in pencil."

Bensington tore a piece of paper out of his note-book and handed it to him.

"That will do," he said. And thereon the young genius wrote:

"My masterpiece, the '*Ame Bourgeoise*.' It is my masterpiece—my masterpiece."

"There, if you will sign that," said Bensington carelessly, "that will remind me of it, and I'll put it somewhere safe away."

The pencil was just going to write the name de la Garne by way of reminder, but Bensington thought better of it.

"No," he said, "don't put anything more on that bit of paper. It'll do very well. I've got a very good memory."

And so they parted: and next day the contracts were duly drawn up and the arrangements made for the package and insurance of that invaluable parcel of canvases for King Street. And the great dealer shook hands again. He first shook the strong young healthy hand of the girl, then next, well balanced as he was, he felt a sort of shudder in the grasp of what he knew, now better than ever, to be the hand of a dying man.

Returned to England, Bensington worked at the clue. De la Garne was impossible. He tried Lord de la Garenne, writing himself to Hampton Warren and getting nothing for his pains but a stiff letter back from the secretary, saying that his Lordship knew nothing about the business. He tried Sir James Dilligan, who had been in the Paris studios in his time, and on receiving an ambiguous reply, was at the time and expense of going all the way down to Cornwall to see the man himself. He was a good deal disgusted to find that Sir James not only had no Bourrot, but that he had got him down with the idea of selling him some rubbish. Then he thought he had it. It was Dalziel Locharne—after all, " *Deel-Locarn* sounded more or less like " de la Garne." And Dalziel Locharne had been a bit of a Bohemian. But Dalziel Locharne, who was a peppery man, lost his temper and told Henry Bensington plainly that if he *had* got any of that modern rot he would have burnt it long ago.

The clue came apparently by pure luck—but then, tireless perseverance gets the luck. It came one evening (he had not been back from Paris more than about a week), when he was dining with Lord Birmingham, the Pailey K.C. of Delgairn's visit to Paris.

"By the way," he said, "you're a picture man, Bensington. What about this man Bourrot they're talking about? It's a funny thing, you know, but I met him when I was with Delgairn years ago. He worked in the same studio that Delgairn had."

And once more did Sir Henry Bensington control his face and leave it as impassive as a bit of wood. He had got the name!

"Delgairn," he said carelessly. "What, the man who has that place down in Warwickshire?"

"Hampshire," corrected Lord Birmingham, and he hasn't got it any longer, poor fellow. He died years ago, after his eldest son, the one who was a cripple. Good lad, but never got on with his father. I ought not to say it, of a dead man too, but I always blamed Delgairn for that. The poor boy couldn't help his hump. And Delgairn never forgave him for not being up to the part. The young man who has got it now—Harry, they call him—*he's* a regular Drury Lane Squire. He's the thing itself. And I think poor old Delgairn died the happier for knowing in whose hands the place would be."

"Ah, yes, of course," said Bensington. "Delgairn's place down in Hampshire——" he waited to see whether he had to push a little farther, but Lord Birmingham supplied him.

"North Merton—it's in the corner there where the three counties meet."

"I've never seen it," said Bensington, as though the

matter were of little interest to him, and they talked of other things; first of poor Bourrot himself—then, as soon as possible, the millionaire was on to other matters which interested him more.

As he walked home (for the night was fine and his house close at hand) he debated within himself whether it would be well to telephone at such an hour. He could easily find out the number from the general directory at his Club. On the one hand, it would not do to miss his chance of the picture by an hour. But then, it would not do to put Delgairn's back up by a summons from a total stranger late at night. He weighed the pros and cons. No. That sort of young beefy rustic (for so he pictured him) was in a better temper in the morning as a rule. And also he could then explain matters properly. At night this sort of clodhopper had a way of being tired, for they lived half the day in the open air.

So it was the next morning, but fairly early—by nine o'clock—that North Merton House was called up and that Sir Henry Bensington took his first step.

He was very careful, lucid and patient. He hooked the young man on, at the other end of the telephone, by talking of imaginary common acquaintances, and of his College, and of how he had heard of one or two drawings at North Merton, Hardings among others. Might he come and see them? And would it be a liberty if he came down? And so on. He got it thoroughly through young Delgairn's skull who he, Henry Bensington, was and what he was, though he did it indirectly. He knew what a very great fortune means in the eyes of such men. It was not a long telephone call—less than ten minutes—but before it was over he had got his invitation, and was to be at North Merton by that evening. And that is what fools call luck; but wise men call tireless industry and organisation.

* * * * *

In North Merton House young Mr. Delgairn awaited his guest.

There was a Prize Boar in North Merton that night (I intend no pun: it was not present in the flesh, it was present in the spirit). It had been a very fine Boar to look at, but it had proved no good for its purpose. It was a failure on the eugenic side. The young squire had bought it in a fit of pedigree mania from a persuasive gentleman who had made a fortune in such things. And, alas! the persuasive gentleman knew more about the business than did Delgairn. It had been four hundred and fifty guineas thrown away—and the railway charge. There had come no progeny, no children to perpetuate and honour the animal's name. He had wanted to go to law about it, but had been wisely restrained. The Veterinary had advised that such misfortunes do befall even the noblest of Sires—among Hogs at least. It had been defined in three leading cases as An Act of God. And now there was the Vet's fee to pay as well. So it was at least £485 thrown away—and Delgairn could not afford £485.

What is more, before they could make sure that it might be but a passing indisposition the virtuous animal had yielded up the ghost, so that it could not even be turned into bacon. The Pig rankled. He rankled damnably. Its former owner and present mourner couldn't forget Samson III. (I'm sorry—I forgot to give you the Dead Champion's name); the more so as he hadn't yet paid for him, and he'd already been dunned twice.

Therefore, when Sir Henry Bensington arrived he felt a frost. His host was in gloom.

But young Delgairn made an effort to receive him properly, and made some kind of conversation at dinner. He heard, in return, of engravings and collectors, but not a figure. He pondered on what might happen, would there be mention later of Twenty Pounds? Thirty? Anything was welcome.

After dinner the two went round at leisure, from room to room.

It flattered the young man to see the interest which the great man showed in the pictures on his walls. The half a dozen good family portraits, one of them a Reynolds, which was an heirloom, and which Bensington examined carefully; another by a local Hampshire man whose name has unfortunately been forgotten, but which was not without talent. There were many water-colours mostly bad, a few drawings, one notable etching, numerous engravings, mainly steel Victorians and a mass of other stuff with no interest to others than the family.

But Bensington stopped a moment before a pencilled drawing of Harding's which was one of the few framed and which had the interest of being dated. He murmured :

"I think I know someone who would like that. Shall I tell them about it ? I hope I am not taking a liberty ? You know, Mr. Delgairn, I took the liberty of thinking you might be considering my offer for one or two things ? "

"Not at all," said Delgairn. "Not at all."

"Hardings in good condition," Bensington went on, peering closely and putting up a single glass before his eye to examine the detail—"—and *this* one is in very good condition—fetch prices nowadays ; not enormous, but I think this man would give £50 for it. Of course, there would be no question of commission."

Then they strolled on. Fifty pounds ! the host's stiffness was notably thawed.

They went along still without haste. They came to the billiard-room—and there Sir Henry saw suddenly (and quickly withdrew his eye)—the Bourrot !

He deliberately went back to look again at an engraving he had passed. Then he strolled back to where the Bourrot hung.

The older man and the younger man stood before the Masterpiece of which the elder knew the value so well and the younger so little. The screen had been pushed aside so that the light from the old-fashioned oil lamps above the billiard-table fell full upon the canvas. There was a long silence ; and Delgairn spoke first.

"It's a Barrett—Burrott I mean. I am told they're worth something, you know."

"Bourrots will always be worth something," said Sir Henry carefully. "But it's only right I should tell you that they are falling in value. Bourrot is still a young man, and he turns out a prodigious amount."

"Yes. But still. . . you know. . ." hesitated the young squire, with the simple cunning bred of dealings in Pedigree Stock.

"There is no reason why he should not live another fifty years," answered the great art dealer quietly. "He is in robust health and horribly prolific."

"Well, you know best."

Yet another critical moment had come in the Art Dealer's fate. His wealth had not dulled his age. Never in all in his long and splendid career did Sir Henry Bensington miss such moments. He said, even more quietly than before:

"I am afraid I can't offer you more than £500 for it."

At those words—"five hundred pounds"—Delgairn's whole being was shaken as though by the explosion of a shell; but his Public School training stood him in good stead. He did not turn a hair. Outwardly his impassive face seemed to say, "Five hundred? Well, let me consider it a moment." Inwardly, his living soul was shouting, "Samson III. settled! No more dunning! Clinch, boy! Clinch! Leap to it! It's too good to be true! The man's mad. Clinch! Don't let go! Hold, boy, hold!" So after a new pause, he said stolidly:

Sir Henry Bensington making a firm offer to a young man of Territorial Rank

"Very well, Sir Henry—but upon two conditions, if you don't mind. You may think me odd, but I don't pretend to be a rich man, and . . . well, one never knows what will happen in this life, does one ?"

"No, one doesn't," answered the other quietly, putting his hands in his pockets and leaning slightly back. "Yes, any conditions, in reason."

"Why, Sir Henry, my only conditions are these. I want you to take the thing with you when you leave—to-morrow morning," he added with clumsy courtesy—"because I am going off myself at ten to shoot with Tommy Menzies—it's a long drive, and I don't want there to be any muddle about the picture with the servants after I'm gone."

"Certainly," said his visitor, without a smile. "I'm catching the 9.20 to town myself." He fully grasped Delgairn's transparent motive for clinching. It was his dread lest something else might go off as well as the picture if this great person from the commercial world had the freedom of his house while he was away. "Certainly, Mr. Delgairn, certainly. I'll take it up to my room to-night and keep it with me to-morrow morning. And the next condition ?"

It cost Delgairn an effort. But the thing had to be done.

"The next condition, Sir Henry," he said, looking frankly into his eyes, "is that you shall give me your cheque this evening."

"Of course," said Henry Bensington in the most

natural way in the world. "It will be simpler if I give it you now, won't it? I have a cheque-book on me." With admirable discipline he again prevented himself from showing even the ghost of a smile.

He leaned over the billiard-table, took out the fountain-pen from his evening waistcoat, and made it five hundred and fifty guineas; nor were the extra five hundred and fifty shillings lost upon the recipient. There was something like gratitude in Delgairn's unemotional tones as he received it, waved it for a moment in the air to dry it, and shoved it with affected carelessness into the breast-pocket of his dinner jacket.

He had made good over the prize boar!

CHAPTER V

Henry Bensington was always in time: but on this occasion he had only just been in time. The first news he saw in his newspaper as he travelled up to London next morning with the Bourrot comfortably tucked away beside him was a paragraph in his *Daily Telegraph*, not largely displayed, but calculated to catch his eye immediately. It told him that "Monsieur Bourrot, the well-known French artist" (it is not my phrase, it is the newspaper's) was lying seriously ill at the *Clinique Sarrel* in Paris. That paragraph had caught his eye before his train stopped at Guildford. Before it got to Waterloo he had made his plan.

Bourrot would not die (it might be presumed) off-hand. It was his experience that these geniuses, though they died young, usually took a few days in dying. He decided to be in Paris the next morning, not that night. And he spent the afternoon in close consultation with Lord Borstal and with Sir Charles Holloway, who had been called in to make a third.

The headlines were decided upon and the main steps of the boom. Sir Henry would bring back or send back by air a photograph of the dying man, of the famous studio in Paris, and if possible, a sketch of Bourrot himself on his bed of sickness. Meanwhile, he would provide a negative of the paper on which Bourrot had spoken so passionately of "His Masterpiece! His lost Masterpiece!" He had it with him, now, in London. Also an old photograph of the Master. The Masterpiece itself he proposed with perfect courtesy not to have reproduced yet. If they would send one of their photographers round to his house with the apparatus for the light and everything, they could have the stuff before dinner.

He was even at the pains, was this Napoleonic man, to advise on the captions, and such was his prestige that even these masters of publicity humbly accepted his phrases rather than their own.

The details of the plan of campaign he left to them; but the main lines were organized and settled before six o'clock. The next morning there was to be a column, heavily leaded, in *The Howl*, and making out the great artist in his imminent danger of death to be the supreme figure of the world. It was the easier to do as not one London man in a hundred had yet heard of him. Bourrot's words on the Masterpiece was to appear in *The Howl*.

For *The Roar* was reserved the old photograph of Bourrot. There was to be a strong protest against the exaggerated deference paid to foreign talent. Bourrot's work was to be discussed in two columns, admitted to be of very high standard, but not so great as that of Mr. Byng, the Tite Street Symbolist and author of the Frescoes in the New Terminus, or that of Mr. Mangus the new voice from South Africa. It would be a tragic day indeed when our mighty empire could not produce oil work superior to that of dying Europe.

All great generals study elasticity of plan, for the future can never be quite accurately predicted. The uncertain element was the exact moment at which Bourrot would die, and the boom must not begin too early. But already before their conversation had begun Sir Henry Bensington had arranged for a telephone call to Paris (what a man !). He had received the report that forty-eight hours would see it all over. Sunday would intervene. Lord Borstal would see to it that there should be a huge display in his three Sunday papers, the Dirty One, the Conservative One and the Liberal One. Sir Charles Holloway would see to it that a full page should be taken up in the Labour One, the Sporting One and the Pious One, with more denunciation of all this exaggerated talk about foreign artists ; and he would have the blocks of the two best-known pictures, the "*Néant*" and the "*Amour Perdu*," (alluded to also as "*Ah me, the Years !*"). He would also have a picture of Mr. Pucker who had bought that canvas, and of Mr. Grant McCabe who had sold it. He would order an article to be written in the Sporting One by his best hack, and Lord Borstal, moved to competition, promised that *his* main article, making out Bourrot superhuman, should proceed from the pen of his most famous Bishop, who would deal with the matter in the Dirty One upon the moral as well as upon the æsthetic side. He should have orders to discuss the possible future of Bourrot's soul, and also to enlarge on the very interesting question whether souls have a future, and whether indeed there are such things as souls at all, in all which matters the Right Reverend Father in God could argue admirably upon either side.

When these things had been accomplished, Henry Bensington took the night train, and early the next morning appeared at the *Clinique* where Bourrot lay.

You may have gathered by this time that our great patron of modern art had nothing foolishly sentimental about him; but he was shocked when he saw what a change had come over the creator of "*Le Néant*" and of the Great Masterpiece. There was still gratitude in the terribly shrunken face and the awfully luminous eyes, and the painter was able, with the damp hand of death, to express by a pressure how strong the gratitude was. He whispered:

"The Masterpiece? My Masterpiece?"

"I have found it," said Henry Bensington, speaking the truth with the simplicity which is always so telling when truth is not squandered but only used upon the right occasion.

Something as near a smile as Death could allow appeared on the fallen features of the artist. He put forth his hand as though to prophecy, saying huskily:

"Mark me, mark me! . . . for untold years. . . ."

Then his voice sank, nothing but a murmur could be heard, his eyelids fell, and he could attend no more. The nurse beckoned. Sir Henry left the room on tiptoe.

Deep Christian Charity of Sir Henry Bensington attending the death-bed of Genius

On his way out from the *Clinique*, which was near the Observatory, he passed the telegraph office of the Senate, opposite the Luxembourg. He sent a couple of telegrams to make sure, and then from his hotel telephoned at length to Lord Borstal. He repeated the exact words: "Mark me! . . . for untold years." He gave as close a description as he could of the scene, so that Lord Borstal's chief draughtsman could depict it with that vigorous pencil so familiar to us all—or at least to those of us who read any one or all of Lord Borstal's three Sunday papers.

Next morning it was as Henry Bensington had expected; the news came to him early, brought to his hotel by a respectful messenger. Bourrot was dead; and he knew enough of the stiff Continental conventions *not* to come back at once to London, but to wait for the funeral, to follow it bare-headed, and to listen with bowed head to no less than fourteen interminable speeches, upon the loss which France had suffered by the passing into the Unknown (not the *Néant* this time) of her immortal son.

He had a right to be there, had Henry Bensington. He might almost have been Chief Mourner, instead of that poor little Adorer (who, by the way, had been regularly married—yes, in Church—and was received everywhere), for had he not provided, all in all, something like sixteen thousand pounds, on which the memory of Bourrot was kept alive for nearly a dozen years. And the little woman who loved him so well was kept alive for more than forty-seven (in a very small villa by the river near St. Germains).

But as for Bourrot, he is in Père la Chaise, and will there remain.

* * * * *

Henry Bensington flew back to London on the day after the funeral, and as he went through the skies the many-sided man mused upon human fame, the unknown doom of the Soul, and things of that kind : but when he got to London, he settled down to business.

He found a sheaf of papers waiting for him ; the Sunday papers of the Great Twins, Borstal and Holloway, the morning papers of the same, the evening papers of the same, the provincial papers of the same, the highbrow reviews of the same (a little behindhand with their news, for they had gone to press only a few hours after he had left London). And He found it all Very Good.

The boom was spouting, gushing, and roaring. The British people were intoxicated with the name of Bourrot, with hints at the Mysterious Masterpiece, with actual reproductions of the glorious "*Néant*" and of the triumphant "*Amour Perdu*," and once more with the picture of Mr. Pucker, purchaser of the same, with the pictures not only of the outside of Bourrot's house, but of the hearse and the six black horses, and the President of the Republic (or some politician or other) speechifying over the grave ; and, what was really a clever scoop (one of Lord Borstal's serfs had got this), of the humble house in which Bourrot had not been born (a splendid farm and steading of the Champagne), under which was the caption, "Humble House in which the great artist was born—typical of the French peasantry." While in the column next it was a reproduction of Millais's "*Angelus*" and "*The Man with the Hoe.*" The serf had also had instructions to snapshot Bourrot's father and mother, during the funeral, but having lingered too long over his consummations he had missed them. They were replaced by two pictures of Auvergnats in costume, bought in the Rue de Rivoli, and labelled: "Parents of the Great Artist—Typical French Peasants."

So much for all that. The field was ploughed, and cross-cut and harrowed. Now it must be sown for the harvest.

* * * * *

There dwells in Golders Green, under the Northern stars, a little man, close on fifty, who dresses carefully but with great strain, for he is very poor: sad in the face, clean-shaven, save for a little drooping moustache; a teetotaller from youth, and possessed of a small library —very little hair, but what there is nicely parted and oiled. His library consists of *Who's Who*, the *Peerage*, Lady Bohun's *Etiquette Book*, the *Red Book*, the *Telephone Book*, and *Whitaker's Almanack*, and also the *Year Book* of *The Howl* (of which he is part author—it is a perquisite. It adds to his little salary, God bless him!).

He works hard under the iron rod of a formidable wife, spare, meagre and with vinegar in her blood. Though she has borne him no children, she insists upon an income—and she is quite right. It pays the rent of the Garden City residence, the joint-a-week, and the wages of the lady help (whose father also is a gentleman of the neighbourhood, but we can't be bothered with his profession).

Yet is this man, hard-working though he be and a docile, not to say bridled, saddled and bitted husband, but half a man. For he is only half of the famous "Lothario," who signs those wonderful Social Paragraphs in Lord Borstal's paper *The Howl*, under the daily caption of "*Among the Smart*."

The other half of Lothario is quite another kettle of fish. He is a hirsute personage, about thirty-five years old and looking any age; abominably slattern. He has a very short little anyhow goat beard, the hair of his head anyhow, a nose already large but getting larger towards the end, and rounded: where also it is red. He is careless about his clothes—and his boots were the worst part of him; he was saggy at the knees—bibulous of eye—having an enormous capacity for liquor of every kind; and as for Holy Matrimony, he has a wife who ran away from him fifteen years ago, another from whom he ran away just afterwards, a third who left him with his best friend, and whom he sees from time to time at dinner—but not a fourth. He has ceased to be domestic. He has a room high up off

Dual Nature of Lothario, Society Journalist

a court at the back of Fleet Street, and instead of keeping to one public-house, as do most of our experts upon what was once Society, he goes the round of a dozen. It is to his credit that, on the whole, he prefers beer to spirits—but nothing comes amiss to his gullet.

And the two together, I say, are Lothario, half and half. Between them they furnish those paragraphs by which we are kept in touch with our Betters. Both enjoy the munificence of Lord Borstal. The Golders Green half, on the one hand, has a weekly salary of £7 10s. 0d., which is given to him in a little square called a "pay envelope" on Friday afternoons. The Fleet Street or public-house half, on the other hand (his employer having long ago despaired of anything regular about him), is on piece work, wherewith I have known him to net as much as twelve solid pounds in three short days: for he is capable of enormities, and he also does find out some things. What is more, he has a cunning trick of holding them up until he knows what the sub-editor will pay.

Now the Golders Green half of Lothario had strict orders from the Chief himself (it was a high honour) to produce two paragraphs on Bourrot. The Chief knew his man, and the Golders Green Lothario was the sort of conscientious fellow who would look up all the facts about that Immortal Genius, so recently dead and buried; but the Public-House Lothario (of whom the sub-editor was a trifle afraid) had a more general commission. He was to let out the great secret that

Bourrot long ago had painted a Masterpiece, which he loved beyond any other of his canvases, and that the great Sir Henry Bensington had bought it, and that it was called "The Bourgeois Soul," exposing with symbolical but fiery satire the shame of that vile abstraction. It was his to explain to the many-headed, the two million who got their own souls from *The Howl*, why artists hate Bourgeois, and what Bourgeois means, and how they hate 'em, and so on.

And the Golders Green Lothario had to do it all in the day's work; but the Fleet Street Lothario had bargained for ten bob a par. And he got it.

Therefore did Henry Bensington when he opened *The Howl* the next morning at Breakfast, read to his great satisfaction in the column "*Among the Smart*" the following sections:—

"*A Modern Leonardo.*

"One hears a great deal nowadays of the decline of art and civilization generally, from highbrows who are themselves incapable of any work. What will they say, I wonder, about this very great Frenchman Bourrot, in ten years' time? A great critic of my acquaintance who for years was the chief name upon the *Civilta* of Florence told me years ago, when we met in the Amerigo Palace in Venice at the table of that charming host—now, alas! dead—Prince Giovanni Amerigo, that there was in Paris at that moment a man who had eclipsed Leonardo. I confess

I had not heard the name, but I have had good cause to remember it since that conversation. It was Bourrot.

" *Though a Frenchman.*

" We are not accustomed to expect much from the French nowadays, especially since their deplorable breakdown during the Great War (as has been well said, they were saved once and they were saved twice, but they cannot be certain of being saved a third time), but even their most pitiless critic will admit that Bourrot was an exception. That phrase 'the modern Leonardo,' strong as it is, is not too strong. And yet he was only a peasant's son, born less than thirty-two years ago, poor fellow, in a little village of that Champagne district (where the wine comes from), and entirely self-made. Of late years he acquired a great circle of acquaintance in Paris and London. It is sad to think that we shall see no more work from his brush."

So much for the Golders Green half of Lothario. There followed the Fleet Street half—but nothing to show the difference in authorship.

" *A Great Connoisseur.*

" I met Sir Henry Bensington yesterday strolling in the Park. He tells me that he has had the good luck to get hold of several Bourrots, and that the most famous of all, the one the Great Master called 'his Masterpiece,' painted in the most masterly fashion and with unequalled mastery, while the master was still young" (in this phrase I am sorry to say that beer began to tell, but the sub-editor put it right) "fell into his hands almost by accident only the other day. But if any man is worthy to possess it, it is Sir Henry, who is admitted on both sides of the Atlantic to be not only the greatest patron of art, but the most acute critic in the art world. Sir Henry Bensington, by the way, is fifty-two years old next Thursday—congratulations!

"*The Masterpiece.*

"As for the Masterpiece, I have been privileged to see it, though wild horses will not tear from me what it is like. But I can tell you the title. It is called the '*Ame Bourgeoise*,' which we may translate in England by 'The Middle Class Soul.' You know, in artistic circles in Paris the word 'Bourgeois' stands for common-place and vulgar taste, and not (as it does with other continentals, such as the Russians), for Capitalism in general. But that is another story, as Mr. Kipling says."

Henry Bensington laid the paper down, well pleased. That was the stuff to give 'em! He took up the telephone, asked for an appointment with Lord Borstal, got it from the servant for luncheon that day, and at the lunch made further progress. The highbrow sixpenny weekly in that nobleman's control had a fierce attack on Bourrot resulting in a shower of letters, both of protest and of agreement. Holloway's press issued a sort of apology for the attitude they had taken, admitting the greatness of Bourrot, but still protesting against the exaggeration of foreign genius, and saying that they had heard that the "Come-to-Britain" movement . . .—the rest of the leader was about our provincial hotels being the best in the world.

These things have got to be very nicely calculated. If you carry them too far in mere bawling, without feeding the public with something more solid, you may get a slump before you know where you are. So Lothario got orders to announce that Sir Henry Bensington was going to show that Missing Masterpiece—Bourrot's young triumph, so long hidden from the world—at Martin's in Bond Street. First he thought he would have a private view by invitation, and the cards for it sent principally to Chelsea. It was that half of Lothario living in Golders Green who was ordered by his stern paymaster to get up the details of time and place and charges of admission, private view and the rest of it. It was the gayer spark in Fleet Street who was implored rather than ordered to prepare a picturesque account of the vision about to be afforded to the eyes of the public and the great craftsmen and craftswomen of Chelsea in a private view.

This second dig of the spur did more even than was

Enthusiasm of Chelsea in the presence of the Masterpiece

expected of it. Chelsea went mad over the "*Ame Bourgeoise*," and fought and squeezed against it in the private view. If it had not been protected by a brass rail the invaluable thing might have suffered damage—and the tragedy will not bear thinking upon. By the time it was staged at Martin's, two days later, all wealthy London and the parasites of wealthy London, and all the artists, and all the writers (poor fellows !), and a good third of the suburbs, were raving about the Masterpiece. Bond Street is not a good street for queues, but Sir Henry was a man of power, and the police permitted one. It stretched outside Martin's all the way down to the corner, and round the corner into Bruton Street, and almost to Berkeley Square. And it waddled in like a worm being swallowed by a bird, hour after hour, although it was two shillings and sixpence per head to see the Masterpiece.

Certainly Henry Bensington had staged the thing well, as he did all things well. The great inner room of Martin's was draped entirely in dead black, with black hangings hiding the ceiling, black carpet, black coverings for the rails. Black everything, except at the skylight. And at the end, absolutely by itself, on the huge void of darkness, hung that little piece of immortality, the "*Ame Bourgeoise*," proving that Art can survive, even in modern times. Under it, in a great Mourning Frame of ebony, was the pathetic pencilled line in the dead man's own hand : "*My Masterpiece ! My Masterpiece !*"

Sir Henry Bensington's humble friend—the same who had made bold to criticize his views on the Claude years before—next wrote to *The Times*, on the fifth day of the Exhibition, while the thousands were still pouring there, to say that in his humble judgment the "*Ame Bourgeoise*" had been hung the wrong way round. The Eye—or rather, what the public in its innocence thought looked like an Eye, ought not to be at the top left-hand corner, but at the bottom left-hand corner: in other words, the "*Ame Bourgeoise*" ought to be hung sideways, not up and down.

Henry Bensington wrote a warm letter defending his own judgment in the matter as a strong Side-ways-ite, and the greatest names in England, or at any rate the greatest names in that department (for the Racing Men fought shy of it, and so did the National Sporting Club) took sides. Lord Stagger, an admitted authority, was an out and out End-on-ite; Philip Bilk, the writer, was a moderate Side-ways-ite; but Rosa Gabble, who has influence with the new generation, said it ought to be hung up by one corner.

It was at this moment, when the enthusiasm was at its highest, that the inevitable happened.

Verecundia, Fifteenth Marchioness of Norbolt, Twenty-first Countess of Pulborough, Thirty-third Baroness Workup in the County of Northumberland and Lady Paramount of Puffin Island, approached the Great Master of the Art World and made a bid.

In vain do you tell me that ladies do not announce

themselves as the nth Marchioness, umpthy-umpthth Countess, and so on, but that only the male of the species enjoys that privilege of ticking off that series upon his fingers. All I can tell you is, that is the way in which Verecundia described herself. She revelled in it.

But Verecundia merits a full introduction, and I will proceed to give it you.

CHAPTER VI

Verecundia, Fifteenth Marchioness, etc., κ.τ.λ, derived, as her name implies, from the exotic regions. She was mainly of the Blood indeed; she was of the Nordic breed and of the island race, for all she knew or I know or anyone else knows. For her late father's name—or that by which he had been last known in life—was Wugg. Her mother's origin is forgotten, but from the daughter's appearance some maintain that the forgotten lady must have had in her some rich southern strain. Yet was Verecundia not of British training. This father of hers had acquired his colossal fortune through the exploitation, rather than the discovery, of the Manium deposits in the Paramooka Islands of the Pacific, at a moment when he was passing under the name of Wonks, though there were earlier friends who gave him another name sounding more like Malchedo. But the world in which he continued to move is not in the way of asking questions.

It is enough for you to know that after he had died worth twenty millions, and after his energetic sole daughter and heiress had burst upon London, Paris, the Riviera, and Deauville, no questions were asked either. She had the only two things needful, the second of which is a masterful mind, though perhaps I ought

Verecundia, Fifteenth Marchioness of Norbolt, Twenty-first Countess of Pulborough, Thirty-third Baroness Workup in the County of Northumberland

to add a third—for a woman of her age—which is good health. She was as strong as a horse.

As to the Marquis, we need not trouble about him. He went off the mortal stage ten years ago, and his son and heir was still at Eton. Managing though she was, and energetic though she was, and even over-bearing, the great strapping woman was not unkind, and she deserved her friends quite as much as she purchased them.

Her two constant friends, the Supporters (as it were) of her Coat of Arms, had reason to know that kindness. It only took the form of capricious gifts; there were no settlements and no capital sums; but they were very well paid for what they did, and she had the sense to choose them from her late husband's immediate world.

The youngest, a child of thirty-three at the most, and girlish at that, was known among her equals—that is, among the rich—though she hadn't a bob—as Ardee. She had derived that loving pet name from a simple jest—she had given a cheque at a bridge party once, just before Lady Norbolt had appeared on the scene, or indeed had come to England at all, and when she had only just come out: and the cheque had been returned —"Refer to Drawer." However, it was all right. She became attached to the great fortune within a year, and was able to pay the money back. It must be admitted that Verecundia was glad of Ardee's support, for Ardee's grandfather, the Bishop, had been the younger brother of Lord Norbolt's father, and Ardee was allowed to call the Dowager, the Dead Peer's surviving mother, Grannie, which was a great privilege, for really she was only grand-aunt. She was, however, of the authentic Norbolt, or rather Walburton, blood (for I need not inform a lady with your knowledge of the world, dear reader, that the family name of the Norbolts is Walburton).

The elder companion had been known as Elless for many years by the same said equals, the One of Us, or whatever you like to call the rich world. She also had not a bob, and that was where the simple jest in *her* case came in. An elderly, angular woman, she had spent the better part of a bitter youth talking so much of L.S.D. that they nicknamed her after that fashion, but called her L.S., or Elless, because she hadn't a penny. It was a shame, for she was a genuine Bailey, being the niece of that same old and still vital dowager Lady Norbolt who had survived her elderly son these ten years, and bade fair to survive him for fifteen more. The Baileys, excellent in blood, had never been rich, and poor Elless had started with nothing but a lump sum of £10,000, which she had promptly lost in Rotheim Deeps, on Billy Dagg's advice during the South African rush, in the days before the flood.

So there she was supporting Verecundia, Fifteenth Marchioness, etcetera, and being supported in turn; and so was little Ardee, and between them they were called the Two Dees; and they followed Verecundia about whithersoever she went, and did all the donkey work, each in her own way.

The life of Verecundia, Fifteenth Thingumbob, should have been perfect. At least twenty millions of money (some people called it twelve, but they were wrong), health, as I have said, plenty of guts (if you will excuse the expression), not a bad heart, and full of a zest in living which made her run after things like a hound. But there was a fly in her ointment. The fly was a bitter one; and yet to hear his name you would never have guessed that there was anything troublesome about him. He was (stand by for it) Hardham, Duque de Emonsillado y Palomar y Manuada y Bo. He lived disgracefully in the worst world of Under-Paris, Under-Monte Carlo, Under-Biarritz—drenched in the air of Whisky, Fizz, New Packs of Cards every night, touts, horses and the Very Bad.

And how did he come to have anything to do with Verecundia, or Verecundia with him?

Alas! it is but too simple! His father, of whom so little is known that I cannot even tell you his name (but at any rate he was of the English-speaking world, and presumably an emigrant from somewhere in it to the Pacific) had been the partner of Verecundia's father, the deceased Wugg (alias, etc., etc.) in their bold adventures, first in the South Seas, later in share shuffling, later still in the grave, and now for all I know in whatever place receives financiers so great and above all so sudden.

Hardham, Tenth Duque de Emonsillado y Palomar y Manuada y Bo. (In the peerage, partly of Castile, partly of Aragon)

And why, you ask, did the son of this other half of the millions bear that high-sounding name?

I will introduce you to something which perhaps you do not know, but which is perfectly true. If you are a man, and you marry a woman with a Spanish title, you become of the rank and of the privileges of the same. If you marry a Spanish Duchess, you become a Spanish Duke. And that was exactly what Hardham had done. Hardham what? Well, as I've told you, no one ever knew: but Hardham son of the Partner of Wugg and playmate as a boy of Verecundia as a girl, in the Coral Islands of the western seas.

When the old lady met him (it was in a gambling hell rather than a casino) she had seen fit to make the match. In England we should have called it a Romance of the Peerage. For Hardham, then not thirty and throwing his millions away, still had the furtive look acquired during his dead father's earlier, less luxurious days, while the Duquessa was seventy-two. She died and left him in lonely state, Grandee of Spain and hereditary Introducer of Ambassadors to the Presence.

With us, I say, that marriage would have been a Romance of the Peerage, but in Spain, where they are more old-fashioned, it had the singular effect of preventing her going back home. They made it too hot for her—and for him. So there he was, twenty years before this admirable story opens, and already Duque de Emonsillado etcetera, with the right to wear his hat before the King of the Two Worlds in the Palace or even in the Escorial; but under this unfortunate drawback, that there were orders to arrest him should he pass the frontier—for the Court would stand no nonsense, and they had a record against the poor fellow.

However, they could not touch his money, and that was the principal thing. Thus he had all that he wanted, by way of a splendid Hotel in Paris, and by way of a little marble palace on the right side of Nice, and away from the noise; and a huge big house in Belgrave Square. But to this last he hardly ever went, for when he came to London he preferred to take a whole great string of rooms in whatever was the noisiest and most expensive hotel of the moment.

And the reason that he growled about coming to London, and that when he went there he stayed defiantly in hotels, was this:

Verecundia, or Vurry, as he obstinately called her, had given him away. It was abominable of her, and it rankled to the depths of his heart.

Hadn't they known each other since they were kids? Weren't it his own poor old dad had helped Vurry's old bonehead of a father over the stile when he had come out of jail, and saved him from being put away again? Even if she didn't want to meet him, she might let him alone. But she had been pitiless, and, as human beings will, she excused herself to herself until she almost made her heartlessness a virtue. The man was impossible. If she once recognized him simply because they had been together in their teens, he would make her life intolerable He might have come straight out of a low dive. He had a crust on him *that* thick—and Verecundia, in her intimacy, would express the thickness of the crust by a gesture of an indignant finger and thumb.

He ought to have climbed into the London rich through Vurry; instead of that, Vurry had thrust him off the ladder, and he was justly embittered. The reader will perhaps hardly believe me unless she has as much acquaintance with the corrupt heart of man as I have, but it is heaven's own truth that there are some men who, however rich, cannot get through the gates in London. They are just too much for the stomach. I am afraid the Duque de Emonsillado was one. I assure you there really are such men. I could name you a living one now whom you have all heard of, only I daren't do it for fear of going to prison. Yet I am not sure that in the sight of his Maker poor Hardham's soul was not a notch or two above Vurry's—though of course, being a man, he had not trained his accent as well as she had (somewhat imperfectly) done. He did not pretend to refinement. He did not pretend to anything, expect anything, but to look after his money—and also to knowing when he had been ill-treated. And if ever one fortune could be used against another, his should be used against the adamantine Vurry.

There was one phrase of hers which had been repeated to him when first he had tried to mix with London, and which he had never forgotten. It was that in which she had warned the world of him by the title of *Rastaquouère*. Oh! It had hurt! It was one of the few dago words he knew—and there was dreadful truth in it. He had retorted (to his intimates) by applying the title *Canaille* to the lady, but it had cut no ice. The only way he knew the word was that his defunct wife had applied it to him once a little before her death when she threw a plate at him—and so he thought it must mean something unpleasant.

At any rate, there things stood; and Verecundia queened it over London, while poor Hardham roamed in the outer darkness, trailing his millions among jockeys and croupiers, and card experts, and the exiles of this world. But still, all the time, with a dull revenge in his heart.

CHAPTER VII

WHEN Verecundia made her offer, she did it, as she did most things, in a round and complete way. She was not such a fool as to write, she telephoned; and summoning the younger of the Two Dees, arrived, supported by that busy little woman, at Bensington's house.

It was a little before the time when people of her station in life get out of bed to spend the hour or two that is needed for washing, half dressing, painting their faces, strapping their bodies, putting on all the artificials, and then dressing altogether. She had said that she must have the Masterpiece. And Bensington had told her that he had no intention of selling it. He was quite polite about it. He pleaded that he had a romantic affection for Bourrot's choice canvas. After all, he had been at Bourrot's death-bed. Her answer was that he evidently had no idea of what she was willing to pay, and she came out with the sum, in round words and without hesitation: "£10,000, whenever you like to have it."

"And what is more," she added hastily, as he would have checked her, "you can keep the thing if you like, to show in the provinces for another month or two."

She would give him any amount of rope, if he wanted more than that, but the picture she must have.

"Didn't I say so?"—Ardee was appealed to, and Ardee nodded vigorously, and piped up:

"You'll have to let her have it, Sir Henry."

But Henry Bensington slowly shook his head.

"Well," said the lady, a little pressed for time, and not inclined for it to be wasted, "Ah'm not going to bargain. Ah'll come again, and Ah'll *make* yeh give it me—perhaps Ah could go further than . . ." But Henry Bensington interrupted her—without rudeness.

"It's really no good, Lady Norbolt. At any rate" (for he knew how to do these things), "it's no good just now. I'm feeling too strongly about it just now. Come and look at it with me a minute . . . and I'd like this young lady to come too. The show shut yesterday, and they sent it back to me at once."

She followed him eagerly into the next room, and thence to a small adjoining room which she was curious to note was fastened with an iron door opening to a key on his watch-chain. Within was a safe, which in turn he opened, and as the huge steel hinges swung back, a small shaded globe lit the inside, and there was the "*Ame Bourgeoise*."

He looked at it in silence, with an infinite depth in his eyes. As for his guest, her appetite was rising to a frenzy. She clutched his arm.

"Oh, Sir Henry, Ah must have it! Ah *must* have it!"

It was wonderful, the way in which he made the

corners of his mouth twitch, as though he could barely resist her appeal.

"Yeh know, Ah really would be ready to make it—well, jest 'most anything. Yeh doan know what it means to me!"

Slowly and sadly Sir Henry shook his head.

"You must let me wait," he said. "You must give me a day or two." He let his chin drop on his chest, and stood motionless; then, pulling himself together, locked the safe, led them through the outer iron door, locked that, accompanied them down to the hall (and all the way she was still eagerly imploring); then he said:

"Yes—it's wrong to keep you waiting. Do you mind coming yourself, to-morrow—and this lady, Miss Walburton, too?" (he wanted a witness). "If you will be here by half-past three, and not later than four o'clock (for I have a very busy day), I can give you my answer."

More than that he would not say, and she was grateful enough. He bowed them out.

Three things had settled rapidly into the depths of Sir Henry Bensington's mind during that short interview (all things came quickly to him)—it was the greater part of his success): first, that Verecundia Marchioness of Norbolt had got at the back of her mind something like £15,000. The second was that he could get at least £20,000, if the thing was properly worked. He didn't need it, God knows! But it was his trade, and his enthusiasm, to buy cheap and sell at the best. It was his life. The third thing was that another dig of the spur was needed, another push to keep the ball rolling. He would have to think out that evening before he went up to dress what the stroke should be. And before he slept that night he had made his preparations for it.

As he ruminated upon the mass of stuff on his desk, his eye caught two letters which had come by a later post. He took them up as a distraction, and by a lucky chance they aided his decision, for they were concerned with the great business of the moment. He sat with both of them between his fingers, reading them one after the other by the light of an electric light in a sconce upon the wall.

The first was a very simple one, brief and to the point. It was written in a boyish hand, not too well spelt, with the date made out in full, and the heading of the paper was North Merton House—and it was a mass of abuse. Delgairn had let himself go. How dared he—Bensington—tell him that pack of lies about Bourrot's hearty health and mass production! How dared he snatch that famous thing by a trick for a song! How dared he take advantage of an honourable man who did not pretend to know anything about such prices? He knew *now* from the papers! Everybody was talking about it. He wouldn't stand it. All his neighbours agreed with him. General Sir Arthur Kenley was agreeing with him only yesterday that it was a damned swindle. It was plain theft, and worse than theft; it was worse than cheating at cards. He would expose Bensington. He had a good mind to thrash him soundly before he exposed him. He had already made the dirty trick as widely known as possible. He would have it all over London.

There was a good deal more to the same effect. Sir Henry read it thoughtfully through, filed it, and then sat down at his desk and with his own hand wrote a brief reply, without even troubling to keep a copy:

"My dear young Mr. Delgairn,

"I am old enough to be your father, and if you will take my advice, you will *never* write letters of that sort. Boys do it, I know, and perhaps if I were vindictive enough to drag you into Court your youth might get you off with a light sentence. But in a very few years it would be a most serious thing for you.

"I cannot say more. But if you knew what prisons were like and how our Courts look at criminal libel, I should not be at the painful duty of having to write this letter. I hope we may neither of us hear anything more about it; but of course I must warn you that if you persist, I shall be compelled to take action.

Always very sincerely yours, and with much thanks for your hospitality, to me, a comparative stranger,

"Henry Bensington."

So that was that. He was fairly used to this sort of thing, after twenty-seven years of picture dealing. It is a trade in which people do explode, or rather, in which people on one side of the bargain have a way of exploding. Then he dismissed the matter from his mind. That unconscious process by which genius develops a plan in one matter while it is at work on another had settled his affair. He had discovered the spur that was needed.

He must get the Masterpiece stolen.

It was rather a commonplace trick, but not yet threadbare, and he fully appreciated the simplicity of Verecundia's mind.

He picked up the telephone (his secretary had gone upon an errand), and told them downstairs to put him through to 1469 Pulton. It was the number where his Jackal had orders to be at that hour—and if " Jackal " sounds too harsh a term, I will tell you why I use it.

* * * * *

About Jackals, then.

Every lion has a jackal—at least, so I read in the natural history books of my youth. Perhaps by this time all that has gone by the board. Let us suppose Henry Bensington to be a Lion—then Chas. Goatcher was his Jackal. He paid for the Jackal's wretched room in a gaunt slum tenement, and for the Jackal's bus and tube fares and occasional travelling expenses. He also gave the Jackal, as any decent Lion would, a small salary to live upon. But he gave him no commission, and never paid for piecework.

Now I come to think of it, I am not sure that Jackal is the right name. The French expression, " his damned soul," is better. Chas. Goatcher was Henry Bensington's damned soul; that is, he had to do whatever Henry Bensington told him to do, to run any risk that Henry Bensington told him to run, and to do any dirty work that Henry Bensington told him to do. It is very useful to have a man of that sort about one, and the great of this world, especially those who make their money quickly, have always got one such person on a string, and sometimes seven. Bensington had a number in varying degrees of ability and degradation. This one was the least able but the most sure, and far the most degraded. He was safe for anything.

Chas. Goatcher had not always been Chas. Goatcher. He had begun life as Sir James Maltaine, with the benefit of a long minority, so that when he came of age he had blewed the accumulation of the minority with a rapidity that astonished even those who, attracted by his lovingkindness, helped him in the matter. He was already in his twenty-fourth year before he had got rid of the last farthing, and he was only just past his next birthday when, being pressed by one of the gentlemen who had reluctantly obliged him since his crash, he very foolishly forged the name of another gentleman, also in his set, trusting (as a generous young fellow would) that so good a companion would not prosecute.

But so good a companion did prosecute, being of that sort. The authorities were kind to him, and he only got five years; but he came out a changed man—which shows how powerful a reformatory agent is the penal system of our beloved country. Even his name was changed, and after he had doubled three times on his tracks, Maltaine had ceased to exist and Chas. Goatcher had taken his place.

Henry Bensington had come to hear of him through an agent in touch with the police. It was at the moment when the picture business was first starting, in King Street, half a lifetime ago. Henry Bensington got hold of him, interviewed him, purchased him, and then very cleverly destroyed the scent. It is not often that the police lose their man when once he has been in jug, but this time they had to confess themselves fairly beaten. Their nark was lost to them.

But Bensington was not so foolish as to depend upon Chas. Goatcher's prison record alone. He got a better hold. He saw to it that Chas. Goatcher should be properly tempted and should properly fall, and he had his evidence all ready, photographs and disk, so that when the foolish Goatcher had that evidence presented to him in the privacy of Henry Bensington's inner room at the picture shop, he grovelled and accepted his chains. From that day onward had Chas. Goatcher been Sir Henry Bensington's man, body and soul.

It was a fine feat for a young fellow just starting in business, and still well on the right side of thirty, but, as I think I have said before, Bensington was a giant among men, the very best type of big business man, and that kind of genius shows early.

A novice in the art of Affairs might have blamed Bensington for using one so inferior in talent and habit, for it must be admitted that Chas. Goatcher was not very quick, not very bright, and that whatever initiative he might have had in the three years between his coming of age and his going to Portland he had lost in the double process of being his own father first and a jail-bird afterwards. But on top of that he took to drink. Not only did Chas. Goatcher drink, but he was one of those whom drink transforms. It made him quarrelsome, and it destroyed for the moment what little judgment he had. It gave him, as a rule, a momentary vigour which would have astonished you had you only known him in the sober half of his day. From a weedy, miserable fellow, prematurely old, he became one showing beans—but not to much purpose: usually to no purpose but futile conflict.

A novice, I say, would have wondered why Bensington chose a slave of this kind; but those who know their world will wonder less. It is exactly the right kind of slave for a certain plain, mechanical sort of secret job. The drink makes It (if I may so call the slave) incapable of revolt when It has slept the stuff off and is in the depths of depression again; but it does not make It incapable of fulfilling simple tasks before the regular drinking hour comes round. And, most important of all, the drink prevents anybody else from thinking of using him.

The task Henry Bensington had it in mind to apportion to his Slave was simple indeed. He could be quite certain of the man's sobriety in the early part of the evening, for on the only occasion when he had dared to break the rule Bensington had shaken him with such a terror that he was never likely to break it again. After the agreed hour of five-thirty he could get as drunk as he liked—and Bensington had hitherto never used him later.

When this Faithful Servitor had appeared, at half-past four in the afternoon, the hour to which he had been summoned, he brought out his greasy note-book, and balanced the pencil in his trembling hand, while his Master detailed the brief order:

"Write down!"

He paced the room. Then he began again.

"Write down: The parcel to be taken to my own room, and put under the mattress just as it is, unopened. The door to be kept locked every time I go out, even for a moment, and the door to be kept locked whenever I am in the room."

"I always keep it locked, Sir Henry," bleated the quavering voice of too-much prolonged sobriety.

"Shut up!" snarled Henry Bensington sharply. Then he went on: "To-morrow at . . . let me see . . . at five o'clock sharp, ring up Sir Henry Bensington's private number, giving the name Percival. If Sir Henry Bensington's voice answers, assure him that all is still safe. Do the same the next day and so on until counter ordered. When any other voice than Sir Henry's answers me I am to leave a message that it is all right. If there is any hitch or trouble, I am to come *at once*

Concentration of a Master of Great Affairs: Sir Henry Bensington dictating Staff Orders to a Subordinate

to Sir Henry's office in person. Further instructions will be given in due time. . . . Now, then, read all that out to me."

Chas. Goatcher read it out, in a voice even more pitiful than before, for the fatigue of sobriety was increasing upon him, and it was near his accustomed hour of release.

"Now read it all again."

With a sigh, instantly repressed, the Slave read it out a second time.

"Now shut your note-book, put it down, and repeat me those instructions by word of mouth."

The Slave repeated them. He had got them perfectly.

"Wait there."

He spoke that "Wait there!" very shortly and sternly—as though there was any likelihood of Chas. Goatcher doing anything else! He passed through the iron door, and the key could be heard turning in the lock of the safe. He came back with the "*Ame Bourgeoise*" and set it down before his servant.

"Do you know that?"

Oh, yes, Chas. Goatcher knew it well enough. He had been to Martin's rooms twice during the show—once, if Sir Henry remembered, in order to keep a watch over certain people and the other time to count the hourly entries. Henry Bensington nodded.

"Fix it well in your mind, because I'm going to wrap it up and you're not to see it again for some time, although you are to have the custody of it."

He left the Masterpiece standing propped upon the table before the worried eyes of the unfortunate man, crossed his arms and watched him to see that those eyes should not leave the canvas an instant. He was determined to fix it upon the Jackal's mind like a vivid photographic print.

"You've got every detail in your head?"

"Oh, yes, sir."

"Very well. That'll do. Now give me that note-book!"

Chas. Goatcher handed it up meekly. His Master glanced through the pages just written, tore them out sharply, and threw them into the back of the fire, where he slowly watched them burn. Not till the last scrap of white had burned black and into ashes did he take his eye off that record. Then he turned to the Decayed Gentleman and said:

"Sit there! Don't move till I come back!"

He went out, taking the Masterpiece with him and could be heard moving, shifting frames, and after that rustling paper, in the outer office. He was away quite a little time, and returned with something the size of a rather large book, tied up in two copies of *The Howl*, stuffed round and protected, whatever it was, and not only corded, but sealed.

"There," he said, putting it carefully and solemnly into the menial's hand. "And you know what'll happen if anything goes wrong!"

"Yes, sir," said the other.

For now twenty years he had been able to say that little word " Sir " quite easily—it had galled him badly at first.

" As you are carrying it," Sir Henry said, " I want you to look nonchalant, and rather gay. . . ."

" Nonchalant and rather gay," repeated in a murmur the Faithful Hound.

" You're to look as though what you carried under your arm was of no great importance, and as though you hadn't a care in the world. . . ."

" . . . care in the world."

" You will have to keep up this attitude down several side streets and to note especially if anyone seems to be following you or watching your movements. If they are, you had better whistle, or even hum a tune. . . ."

" . . . hum a tune."

Chas. Goatcher picked up his lanky, now almost fainting form—it was getting near his usual hour. He felt it was hard lines. But it would not be forty minutes back to his room, and then he could relieve the strain, preferably with a Splash—or perhaps, as he was very tired, he would begin with a Double Neat.

And the last words that rang in his ears as he passed through the front door (to which Sir Henry had closely followed him to make sure that the precious bundle was well held) was the menace :

" Look as though it wasn't important ! Look cheerful —whistle ! Hum ! "

CHAPTER VIII

Verecundia, on returning to Norbolt House from her interview with Bensington, was exhausted with emotion. The Two Dees played up nobly. They earned their meals and lodging like Trojan women, and without the miauling Euripidean peevishness of same.

"Dear Verecundia," said Ardee respectfully, stroking the back of the head of the Head of the Family, "you must not let it worry you like this!" Then she added, with the charming girlish timidity of her short thirty odd years: "May I say what I think?"

"O' co-urse, darling!" cooed the Peeress.

"Well, dearest, what I was thinking all this afternoon was this. Have you any need to worry? You know, with a fellow like Harry Bensington it's only a question of what you'll pay. And after all" (a look of glory came into her eyes), "you *can* pay *any*thing, *can't* you, dear?"

Verecundia's mouth became stubborn. She had not only inherited, she had also cultivated, a right appreciation of money. Ardee caught that expression at once, and said:

"Oh, you know what I mean. What I mean is that really, dearest, you can make *certain* of it. It's only a question of guessing his figure, and meeting it."

"What do *you* think, Elless?" murmured the Great

One, turning to the other side, where the Second Dee sat, angular and ready.

"I agree more or less with Ardee."

"Why less?" asked Ardee, protesting across the noble form in her eagerness.

"I didn't mean that," said L.S.D. rather sharply. "What I mean is" (to Verecundia) "that I think a person like *you* will know better than anyone else what is in the mind of that odious man. You see, Verecundia, you've got an uncanny power of reading what is in people's minds—everybody says so. And I'm sure if you'll only externalize as we call it at the Second Church of Christ Psychic—call up Bensington's face before you and his desk and all that—the right figure will appear. It might be under £20,000, or it might be over £20,000; it might be about £18,000, for instance, or £23,000. I don't know, I don't pretend to understand these things. But *you* do, and to be quite frank, you've got a sort of second sight about it. I don't say it's the highest kind of gift, but you've got it. You remember when we bought the pendant of that woman who'd been murdered in Cannes, last year? How you got it withdrawn before the auction?" (Verecundia nodded.) "Well, it's like that now. With all your faults you've got that astonishing gift for fixing things that are in other people's minds, and for seeing the figures in the air. And when you've got his figure fixed, you can startle him by offering just *that*. I think that's the way to do the business," she said. She snapped her mouth.

It was good flattery, for the rich like their flattery with vinegar, and Verecundia was impressed. She found the energy to sit forward a little, took a hand on either side in each of hers. Then she said to Ardee, nodding at Elless:

"She's quite right." And then said to Elless in her turn, "Yeh're quite right." She let go the two hands, pushed her face forward in an idiotic stare and stuck like that for a full thirty seconds. Then in a distant awful voice, sibylline, not of this world, she intoned: "Ah see a wreathing mist . . . it is red . . . smoky. . . . Ah see figures forming . . . £20,000. . . ." She sank back with her eyes shut. A respectful silence surrounded her. She languidly awoke: "Ah've seen it," she said simply and in her everyday tones. "Ah've seen the figures. Shall I tell ye what they are?"

"Oh! Please!"

"Oh! Do!"

Verecundia gratified them.

"He has gotten hid in his mind a large figure: £20,000."

"Dear, *dear* Verecundia," began Ardee — Elless interrupted:

"Offer that £20,000 firm: to-morrow morning, first thing, the moment you get there. Be ready to give it there and then, and he'll fall right off the shelf. That's what I say."

"You're taking me with you, aren't you, dear?" said little Ardee.

"Yes. We arranged that, dear."

Elless said nothing. She would have given a lot (if she had had a lot, but she had not!) to be present at that interview—after all, was it not of her own creation? But long experience had taught her when to be silent. She looked none the more pleasantly at Ardee, all the same.

* * * * *

Verecundia was for bed, though it was early. Ardee attended her to her room with filial devotion, and when she had said good night, came back to Elless with a suggestion.

"We can't go to bed at this hour, Elless. Let's go and stuff the Old Girl. It's a charity. They never unscrew her till about midnight, and even then she'll make that unfortunate Smithson read to her for hours. It'd be a charity to Smithson if we got her sleepy with tit-bits."

"Anything you like," said Elless. And down they went to the very charming little room which the Dowager Lady Norbolt had inhabited for the last ten years—ever since her son's death—whenever she came up from the country to visit her daughter-in-law in state, and to continue the traditions of Norbolt House.

She was overjoyed at the coming of the Two Dees. She thanked them quite sincerely, using the conventional formula of patronage—"Young people" (and with that she lovingly glanced at Elless) "are *really* kind to take the trouble to come and talk to an old woman like me!"

Scandal for the Dowager

She put up her ear trumpet in eager expectation, and she was not disappointed.

"A thousand?" she chuckled. "Well, that's a lot!"

"No, *twenty* thousand—at least—thirty, perhaps!" shouted Elless.

"Nothing dirty about it?" said the Dowager, a little startled, but with a Saturnine smile.

"No—THIRTY, I said!" roared Elless.

"THIRTY!" shouted Ardee in chorus. "Thirty thousand—or more!"

"Thirty thousand?" queried the old lady, leaning forward as well as her aged bones would allow her. Then she sank back. "Oh, nonsense!" she said.

Ardee nodded vigorously.

"Yes—or perhaps *Forty* thousand!

And Elless, who had command of the ear trumpet, supplemented the shock with a new vigorous howl:—

"*Fifty* thousand, perhaps! She's raving mad about it!"

"Well, it's her money," murmured the old lady. "But really, you know . . . fifty thousand!"

Ardee repeated and continued:

"I tell you, she's fairly mad about it, Grannie. We did all we could to dissuade her. . . ."

"Yes," said Elless, with a tragic vibration in her voice. "All we possibly could, dear Lady Norbolt. I appreciate what is due to our family."

At the word "our" the very old lady looked more

sardonic than ever. But all she said was: "Fifty thousand! . . . Well, it's her money."

"He's very famous, Grannie!" roared Ardee.

"No! She's well known, of course—famous isn't the right word," answered the Dowager with dignity.

But Elless commanding the ear trumpet got it right.

"No, not *she*, dear Lady Norbolt—*he*—the man that painted the picture—Bourrot."

"That's French slang for a donkey," said Lady Norbolt, reminiscent of young officers with whom she had danced at the Tuileries in her girlhood.

"Well, at any rate," said Ardee, "he's all the rage. He painted 'Lost Love,' you know."

"Is it at all like Watts's 'Love and Death'?" asked the Ancient.

Elless shook her head:

"It's a sort of zigzag!" she shrieked.

"A wigwag," sighed old Lady Norbolt contentedly. "I don't understand these new terms. Is wig-wagging Yankee for love?"

Then she shut her eyes, as very old people will sometimes, losing her vitality in a sudden access of sleep. The Two Dees looked at each other. Ardee nodded, and touched the forehead under the wig with her lips; and Elless, not to be outdone in courtesy, got at another bit of the forehead in the same way.

"Good night, darling Grannie," bellowed Ardee. "Shall I send Smithson to you?"

"Yes," said the sleepy old voice, and the eyes opened

for a moment. They lit upon Elless with recognition, and then the lids fell again; and when Ardee had fetched Smithson the two went out, with the feeling of a good deed accomplished and of Age entertained respectfully by Youth. Each in turn sought her own small room at the top of the house and bed; Ardee to dream of what it would be like to have Twenty thousand pounds like a sixpence in one's pocket; Elless, taught by experience, to pray for the crumbs that fell from the table, and to waste no energy in dreams.

* * * * *

Henry Bensington, a man of precision, was sitting down at his desk, as he always did, at exactly nine o'clock in the morning. He opened all his correspondence himself, and he read it through before sending for his secretary. He was not of the kind that put themselves into other people's power.

It was not a very large batch this morning, but on one very large envelope with the coloured Blazon of the Plantagenet Hotel (three Leopards Or, on a field Azure, Argent in Pale Reverse, and the blazon "Dieu seul") hugely embossed at the left-hand corner, he saw a very large handwriting that called a smile to his face.

He put it aside till he had looked through all the others. Then he opened it. He had recognized it as the Duque's own hand, the hand of that immemorial line which stretched upwards (through the ladies) to the dim beginnings of Aragon.

It was five years since his last transaction with the

great nobleman, for the Duque of Emonsillado was no patron of Art, and the little favour that Henry Bensington had been able to do him had not been concerned with pictures, but with a spot of blackmail which had to be settled by the good offices of an expert.

He thought to himself, as he balanced the note in his fingers before reading it, that there must be some very special reason for His Grace's wielding the pen himself. It was not an exercise to which he was accustomed. He preferred a machine. And when he opened it, he discovered that reason well enough. His Grace disdained all subterfuge, and went straight for the bull's-eye:

"Dear Harry,

"I haven't seen you for years. But I'm sure yore in the pink. Looke here, you've got to keep that Boujoys Arm for Yors truly. And you no WHY. Name yore own figure. But if I dont get it I'll break things. Dont tellephone. They hear everything. Just send round yor ortograph.

"s.l.,

"Hardy."

Henry Bensington smiled more broadly, nay, to the fullest extent that he allowed himself. Yes, indeed, he did know why His Grace was making that offer, and making it so early! It would have been like the Grandee to have struck the very moment the thing came back from the Exhibition, or even before; but he had been travelling, and he had only reached London the night before and had only heard then the news that Verecundia was after the Masterpiece. He had lost no time! He had written at once and posted before midnight.

So it was the old game of spiting Vurry! Just what Hardham had done two years ago with the Villa, and *tried* to do with the folio at Christie's. Henry Bensington got up, as his custom was when his spirit was stirred, and paced up and down the room.

It was astounding—he thought—and the smile returned with the thought—what a lot humanity will pay for its vices. He had already settled that Verecundia could be screwed up to something close on Twenty thousand, certainly more than fifteen—and now here was that low scoundrel Hardham coming into the market with his millions. Really, he could make it what he liked!

It sounded absurd; it *was* absurd: but upon his soul, he thought he might get £20,000 for the beastly thing . . . if he played his cards properly—and trust him for doing that!

When all these things had passed between Henry Bensington and his own great soul, he sat down and wrote, first a rough copy by way of record, and then, in his own hand and on his best paper, the very brief answer required:

"My dear Hardy,

"I've got your letter, but I have also got bad news for you. The thing has been stolen. The loss was discovered this morning—by me, when I opened the safe. It may be recovered—I don't know. My experience is that in thefts of this kind, either it is traced at once, or never. But I will keep you in touch. Meanwhile, of course, I shall have to tell our Mutual Friend. I can see by your letter that you know she has been after it! Have I guessed right? I have.

"Yours,

"Harry."

Then he rang the bell, and had the letter sent round at once with instructions to his messenger to put it into the Duque's own hand.

Nor were these instructions unpunctually fulfilled. It was eleven minutes to ten when Henry Bensington's messenger presented the thing, as he had been ordered to do, at the splendid Catherine II suite of the Plantagenet, and saw it taken from him by the tall, rather menacing figure which was, at the moment of reception, in shirt-sleeves. It had not yet breakfasted. By ten minutes to ten the door was safely shut again.

It was about nine and a half minutes to ten when Bensington's messenger, waiting by the lift in the corridor, heard a roar of laughter, exultant, enormous, proceeding, hardly muffled, of such volume was it, from the suite so aptly named after the Semiramis of the

North. The noise was the noise of the Duque de Emonsillado y Palomar y Manuada y Bo glorying and exulting in Huge Olympian Mirth. With right fist clenched upon the note he had just read, with left arm triumphantly waving in the air, he continued to shout between his salvos of barking joy:

"Oh, bully for Vurry! Oh, gud, gud, gud, for li'lle Vurry! Lorst? Oh, too gud to be trew!"

And with the other hand, which still held the crumpled message, he pounded himself about in his delight. "Gawd! Ah'd give a dandy bean to see hur face, time she knaws!"

So true is it that pleasure and pain are relative, and that what will make one suffer will make another rejoice (*Marcus Aurelius*). His Grace, dispensing with grace, sat down to breakfast with a better grace than was common to him. He'd been worried since the hour the night before when he had heard that the slanderous Verecundia was panting for the Masterpiece, whether he'd gotten his foot in the door in time—"an' now the gurl was bunkered, and it hadn' cost him a durn bean either!"

But there was no time to be lost. He remembered suddenly that every minute counted. He jumped up from the breakfast-table (only wishing he could trust the telephone), scrawled at top speed the line:

"Wen found, I buy, your price. Mind! H."

Stuck it down in its envelope, and sent it round at once

Inhabitual exuberance of a Spanish Grandee on hearing the Misfortunes of a Rival

to the Master of Modern Art—who in his study read that brief line three times, smiled again the same smile, and then locked it with its earlier fellow in a small private drawer of his desk.

* * * * *

It was not twenty past three on that same afternoon when he was told that Lady Norbolt and a friend were asking to see him. He looked at the clock. He smiled that smile. She was ten minutes before the earliest time he had suggested. It was some driving power which could get a woman *more* than punctual!

Verecundia and Ardee came in. He rose to receive them, and then, although they still stood before him, allowed himself the singular gesture of sitting down again before they did. He put out some papers before him on his desk, drawing upon them with his pencil a few figures, and one or two meaningless signs.

He knew what he was doing. Attitude affects bargaining, and there is a certain degree of low breeding which makes for getting the better in a bargain. Also the conviction that you dominate your opponent by standing up is old-fashioned nonsense. If you are Big Business, you sit at your desk, which is your throne of power.

Verecundia did not like it, but she had not come to quarrel, she had come to clinch; and though her colour heightened at the rudeness, she swallowed her pride, cut out all the frills and came straight to the meat.

"Ah've come to make that offer, Sir Henry, as yeh know, and Ah've made up me mind on it."

He continued to scribble aimlessly with his pencil on the paper before him, to make initials, and to put down figures. His eyes thus cast down did not meet hers, and the severe determination in hers was wasted.

"Ah doan wănt t' waste time," she said strongly. "And Ah doan wănt to higgle. It'll be noh good higgling. Ah've come to make ye a furm offer for £20,000." She motioned to Ardee for her bag. "An' please let me pay it right away now."

Henry Bensington continued to touch paper with pencil. Then he dropped the pencil, put his elbows on the desk, clasped his hands, looked up into her face, and shook his head.

"Ye won't . . ." she began, almost passionately.

"It's not that, Lady Norbolt," he answered quietly. "It's something worse. The '*Ame Bourgeoise*' has disappeared. It has been stolen. . . ."

She turned very white: gave a sharp, rather shocking gasp. She had hardly known herself under what a tension she had lain.

". . . And from what I know of such things," he went on, in the same steady voice, "I'm afraid we *may* not see it again."

Then it was that with a dreadful moan Verecundia Fifteenth Marchioness of Norbolt, Twenty-first Countess of Pulborough, some - thing - or - other - eenth - or - eccond

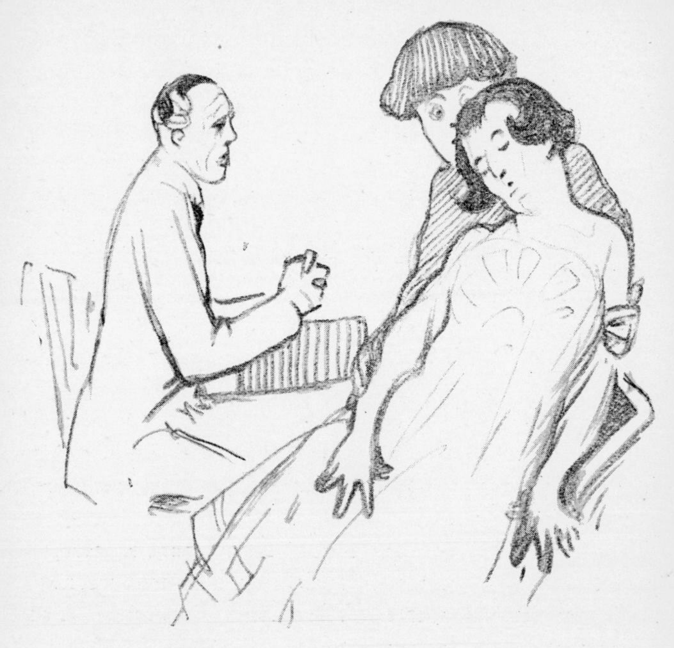

Restrained sympathy of a Master of Great Affairs (Sir Henry Bensington) with a Lady of Title (Fifteenth Marchioness of Norbolt) en defiance

Baroness Workup in the County of Northumberland, sank fainting into her dear dependant's arms.

"Oh, Sir Henry, how *could* you?" wailed poor Ardee, supporting the considerable weight as best she could, and staggering towards a neighbouring chair. "Verecundia, dearest, darling, Verecundia!"

"I'm sorry, Miss Walburton," said Henry Bensington, still with decision, still in a moderate voice, and still remaining seated. "It's not my fault. It's I who stand to lose by this. And it's better to break bad news like this straight out at once."

Then he rose, not too rapidly, came over to where they were, and helped to lift the now barely reviving beauty of the Southern Seas on to the Empire couch under the little Corot. Verecundia's fine dark eyes slowly opened. It all came back to her. She asked for brandy. It was procured. There followed a flood of tears.

"Aw! Sir *Hen*ry," she wailed, "Sir *Hen*ry! . . ."

"You can't be sorrier than I am, Lady Norbolt," said the Master bitterly. "The thing's done."

* * * * *

It was a good half hour before Verecundia could be handed, with infinite pains, Ardee on the one flank, Henry Bensington on the other, the Housekeeper supporting the rear, down the rather steep steps of the famous little house, through the passage, avoiding the shop, into her motor with its nice little crest. Thereinto was she decanted with all the ceremony due to her rank, and the very much more it was necessary to add for her millions, and the transaction was at an end.

After the long rest which such violent emotions needed, she did at last receive a note from Bensington which helped to support her spirit. It was very well put. It did not commit him, and it was friendly. It even went so far as to apologize for his apparent lack of sympathy: "He had trained himself not to show such things, but she must understand that he had been terribly hard hit. He had a devotion for that picture which went to the very roots of his soul—and she must remember that he had known Bourrot, and had sat by him while he was dying." The missive ended with the assurance that if ever it were recovered, he would remember her figure, and discuss it with her. And he oddly used the words: "respectful assurances" before he signed.

CHAPTER IX

You will remember, reader, if that charming shingled head of yours is not a Tête Linotte, how, on that evening when Verecundia was consulting with her Two devoted Dees, Chas. Goatcher had gone out into the evening under the threatening orders to look cheerful, to whistle, and even to hum.

Whether or no he looked cheerful his master would never know. But he did whistle a mournful note or two, and he hummed, till he was round the corner. Once he was round the corner, and free, one single thought possessed him, to get back to his miserable garret, deposit the sealed thing that he had under his arm, and then, for the love of God, a drink! He remembered (for his brain was clear) that by five o'clock of the next day he was to telephone and reassure his master that all was safely under lock and key.

It was a great shame of Bensington to have kept him so late! It was a breach of an implied contract between them—a contract not openly made but taken for granted—that he should always be released before the pubs opened. Yet here he was, with the pubs open this half hour and more, and he still waiting in anguish. He hurried on.

The parcel under his arm was not much, but it seemed heavier with every step—and by this time he had got east of St. Martin's Lane. His control lasted for a little way up Long Acre—then it broke down. It was Bensington's fault, anyhow . . . he would have just One, One wouldn't hurt him! Then he would faithfully go and lock the beastly thing up, and then go out again and get his regular whack. . . .

But why should he wait for that Just One? . . . He was fainting . . . besides, he absolutely *must* have it. He turned into the first common bar he came to, and took it—with a splash. . . . There, that was better! He must have another. No, he must not linger. It was all right, one made no difference. He looked at the parcel under his arm, and then felt it, foolishly, to make certain that it was there, and he hurried on. . . .

But the trouble was that that first one had been quite insufficient; indeed he would have done better, he thought, not to have had it at all, than to compromise like that. . . . He must have a proper drink—and then he would go on with his orders, and lock the abomination up (his arm was beginning to ache, and his shoulder had always hurt him since that rheumatic fever of years ago. . . .). Yes, he would have one more, a good one. . . . And then he would not feel the need of one for some time. . . . In that way he could be certain of locking it up safe, and having the evening free, and that was what he wanted.

He went to the next one that appeared, and he had two quite satisfactory doubles, and then two more. He sat down to it. It made him feel more respectable and solid. And then again, it hadn't done him any harm. . . . The truth was (said Chas. Goatcher to himself) this kind of thing didn't ever do him any harm. He could carry it, he could . . . and he was feeling altogether more himself . . . come on.

He stretched, he pulled out his whiskers a little on each side, he pushed his billycock slightly towards one ear . . . it was grand to feel oneself again! He was a little uncertain as to why he had felt not himself, but he remembered Bensington in the rough, and how he had been bullied.

Then his mind jumped back suddenly to his orders. He clutched nervously at the parcel under his arm and assured himself it was still there. . . . What had he to do with it? Why, to take it back to his room, of course, and lock it up. He remembered all that. And then there was plenty of time. He had to do something or other the next day. . . . He couldn't quite remember what it was—but it would come back to him after he had slept it off. Anyhow, the parcel was safe, but it was damned heavy. . . . And all he had got to do was to take it to his room . . . his room, you know . . . yes, his room. Those were the orders. Lock it up . . . for fear it should run away. He laughed to himself boisterously at the jocular idea . . . a parcel running away! Ha! Ha!

He was a devil of a fellow by the time he came out of this second pub, and took the road again.

He thought a little mews down to the right might be a short cut. He found it was a no-thoroughfare. He came back, and took another turning. He got fairly lost. He leaned against some iron railings and stupidly considered his parcel. He had to take it to his room. . . . the address of his room? He knew that—5 Munning's Rents, top floor, under the roof—which leaked. But it wasn't raining, so that was all right. He must find out how to get to Munning's Rents. They couldn't be very far off.

A small but well-appointed public house stood under a brilliant arc lamp opposite the entry of the narrow alley from which he issued out into the main street. On it in fine flaming letters was the title of that hospitable house, The Butcher's Arms. Surely in so magnificent a place they would know all about their London, and they could direct him easily to Munning's Rents—or someone inside could. . . . Anyhow, he would go inside . . . and inside he went.

There was a pretty thick crowd in the common bar, and it was many years since Chas. Goatcher's finances had allowed him any other department. He squeezed in by the edges of it, and had the luck to find a bench right at the corner of the bar. They were all standing up, and that bench was neglected. Hence his good fortune.

Down went the burden from under his arm—and how

relieved that arm was at the loss of its burden! He rubbed his shoulder. Then a great necessity came upon him. He staggered to his feet, wormed his way through the press of drinking men and a few women talking much too loudly, lurched to the bar, and conveyed the order for a double. He had to say it twice. It disgusted him to observe that the woman appeared to be deaf. He got it at last and began to sip it sombrely. It was the habit of the unfortunate Goatcher, while still he was Maltaine, to pass, in the curve of his inebrieties, from elation to some doubts upon the goodness of the world, and he was now at the doubt stage. He was doubting man's virtue. He was beginning to dislike his fellow-beings. It was usually the last phase but one with him before sleeping it off. The intermediate phase was either maudlin tears or gentle kindliness. But he was now in the thick of the have-at-you phase, and the "Why is the world my foe?"

His uncertain and watery eyes fixed themselves on a man with a squarish parcel under his arm, done up in newspaper. The man was haranguing. He was a man of words.

Mr. Goatcher watched him with vague distrust. Sometimes he doubled into two men and then came together again. That alone was suspicious!

The man with the parcel under his arm was addressing his own group indeed, but also the universe at large, and fatal words issued from his lips. They were these:

"An' wot if a man 'as done time? I don't say as there ain't those 'oo do time as deserve it or those as do time an *don't* deserve it. Wot I ask is, wot if a man '*as* done time?"

The question was rhetorical and emphasized by a wave of the unoccupied hand in the air. A deeper suspicion arose fuming in the muddled brain of Sir Henry's Personal Agent. He glanced darkly at the orator, and sidled up towards him.

Fate, ever on the alert, added another little element to her drama. She caused the rhetorician to glance vaguely at Mr. Goatcher, and as he did so, he asked once more of universal justice and the Gods below: "Wot if a man '*as* done time?"

Mr. Goatcher was on the tremble. He had enough sense left to remember that this was his third public-house. He also remembered, enormously, a charge, a commission, a parcel, done up in newspaper. It *ought* to be under his own arm, a square parcel. It was *not* under his arm. . . . And somebody was insulting him. He pressed his elbow against his ribs and made certain that there was nothing under his arm. He tapped his arm on the outer side, and made doubly certain. He lurched forward and noticed the parcel under the arm of the abomination who had talked about doing time: and he said, suddenly and surprisingly loudly:

"You've got my Thing."

"Your wot?" cried the startled orator.

"Mine. Don' know name of it. That thing under

Altercation between a gentleman who has lost his rank and another Gentleman who has never attained it

your arm. It'sh mine." And Mr. Goatcher made a grab at it.

" 'Ere! You leave that alone!"

"Yus, you leave it alone! D'y'ear?" said a third party, who had nothing to do with the trouble.

"Don't yer stand it, Bill," said a fourth, who wanted to see sport.

Chas. Goatcher tipped his hat a little more to one side and was swollen with the love of justice.

"All ask ish . . . is . . . my own back," he shouted. " 'Tishn't your callor my call. It'sh my own. I want m'own back. I have have it. Under ordersh. Hand bloody over!"

A great fear occupied his opponent's spirit. For to tell you the pure truth (and there is no reason why I should not) that parcel which he carried under his arm done up in newspaper was a silver tray, neatly conveyed from a shelf near an open window which he had had the good fortune to pass earlier in the evening. Bill, the orator, a man who in a higher station of life would have adorned the first ranks of finance, on seeing that tray had acted at once and with decision. He had copped it before you could say Knife! He had wrapped round it a random piece of newspaper which was lying in the street. He had walked off, not too rapidly, yet at pressure. He had bought another newspaper and made the whole thing secure. Now you must know that Bill was in a favourable situation for dealing with silver trays. He was privileged. His brother-in-law, to whom he was greatly attached (and the esteem was mutual) was a Smasher, and had a private crucible. That tray would fetch Bill five florins, and five florins was a fine day out.

But he had no desire to have that tray examined just now. He gave Chas. Goatcher a push.

"Don't you push me," said Chas. Goatcher fiercely. "Give me back parcel!"

By way of answer Bill suddenly dived through the crowd, shot through the swing doors with his paper parcel under his arm and fled down the street.

Chas. Goatcher (so strange are the effects of the Lenean God) would have had difficulty in following him before that last drink, but now he had none. He pounded along heartily. An eager man went first, but a still more eager man came after. In vain did the quarry double and turn, the hunt followed every move; when, just as the burdened man felt the weight beginning to tell, and the pursuer's outstretched hand almost grasped the collar of the fugitive, Chas. Goatcher tripped and fell smack down upon the unfeeling stones of London.

He staggered to his feet, noticed blood coming from his nose, much on his clothes, and some drops of it on the pavement, He leaned against the wall and began to cry softly; for the maudlin stage had come. He blubbered to himself inaudibly. "Murder this time! Murder! There's no end to it!"

He glared with glassy eyes for a full minute as he leant thus, propped up against the wall, at a large advertisement under an electric arc, which implored him to subscribe to the Duchess's fund for the unemployed. That advertisement was vaguely familiar. Hooray! He was at the corner of Munning's Rents.

Bruised, weeping, in the last stages, he staggered up those dirty stone stairs, gripping the iron rail and remembering dully that it was his bounden duty to lock his door. He snapped the key, fell upon his dishevelled bed, and fell into oblivion. In that best of states I leave him, to return to a wealthier and therefore a better world.

CHAPTER X

THE day after his orders to Mr. Goatcher and his sad disappointment of Lady Norbolt Sir Henry Bensington came in to his office very late, after lunching too long with Lord Birmingham at the Ritz. Already had Lord Birmingham heard the news, for little Ardee had told Elless, who had told the Dowager, who had told Smithson, who had told the chauffeur, who had told Lord Birmingham's chauffeur, who had told Lord Birmingham, because Lord Birmingham always liked to hear these amusing little things. Indeed he had begun:

"Strange thing that, m'lord, about Sir Henry's picture!" And Lord Birmingham had been heartily tickled, and had muttered: "Clever devil!" He wondered as he drove back from his lunch whether he might not have to try the case, and he was more amused than ever.

But with Sir Henry Bensington he was sympathetic and charming. He went off to an afternoon appointment, and Bensington went back to his business, buying on the way Holloway's evening paper.

Holloway had been very good. He had done as they had arranged. It was all right. There was the warning (as had also been arranged) the big type about there being unfortunately no photograph of the picture, which made it doubly difficult to trace it. He stopped his car a moment to buy Borstal's evening paper. Borstal had been even kinder. He had made it look like a European war or a murder case. And since there could be no photograph of the picture, there was a photograph of Sir Henry Bensington instead, taken thirty years ago, and doing him proud.

He waited at his office until five o'clock. Everything was going well, and everything would continue to go well. With a punctuality which only well-trained unfortunates are capable of, Chas. Goatcher would come up to the mark. He had never failed him yet. It was five past . . . ten past . . . no telephone. Henry Bensington began to turn over possibilities. Suppose Goatcher had been attacked? Kidnapped? Suppose he had madly gone off with the treasure? No he couldn't be so silly! They'd have him at once!

* * * * *

Half-past five and no message. This was serious. In all these years Chas. Goatcher had never missed. He was always absolutely certain in his hours, before his licensed moment of debauch. Still, one never knew.

Henry Bensington waited till six o'clock struck, and half-past. Then his mind was made up. There was no question of the motor this time. He put on a soft hat, well pulled over his eyes, turned up his coat collar, walked to the Dover Street tube station, walked again form the Holborn station at the other end, and so came to Munning's Rents. He went up those filthy stone stairs—he knew the way; he had done this once or twice before. On the sixth, top, landing, outside Goatcher's open door, through which the miserable bed could be seen, unmade, stood that angry woman the caretaker.

"If you're looking for that man Goatcher, 'e's gawne," was all she said.

"How do you mean—gone?"

"What I say—gawne. I don't know oo you may be—I aven't seen you round 'ere afore."

"I'm the man who sends you the rent," said Henry Bensington quietly. "Poor Mr. Goatcher is a dependant of mine."

It did not mollify her much.

"Well, you can give me the rent now," she said defiantly. "For 'e's taken everything he had—not as *that* were much! E' musta made a bundle of it. There was a shirt, and two pair of socks, to my knowledge, and one pair o' shoes. Ow e's gawn right enough! But e's not taken nothing as wasn't 'is own."

Henry Bensington produced the rent money without a word.

"You can give me no idea at all?" he said, fixing her with his strong eyes. "Don't you know his habits? Don't you know where one might look for him?"

She shook her head as she wrapped the few shillings carefully in a horrid handkerchief, and thrust the packet into the pocket of her apron.

Henry Bensington instinctively took out his pocket-book—and then with quick thought put it back. It would never do!

"Well," he said, "I don't ask you to tell the police or anything."

"I don't want to 'ave nothing to do with the perlice!" said the woman sullenly.

Henry Bensington turned without a further word, and went down those stone stairs in silence, she watching him and divided between the danger of crossing a man who seemed so well-to-do, and the danger of finding herself subject to police inquiries. She decided to do nothing. She waited till she heard his steps go out through the archway of the dingy court and then went back to her own den.

* * * * *

It was about a hundred and fifty yards from Munning's Rents, and perhaps two hundred from the Tube station, that the working of Sir Henry Bensington's brain reached its conclusion.

The whole thing was clear to him, now! It was Delgairn!

There was only one human being who hungered and thirsted for the *personal* picture in itself; not to show it, not to sell it, but to possess it. There was only one person who would want to hold it in *secret* possession for a while. And Bensington knew enough about the human heart to understand with what violence the grievance rankled.

His opinion of Delgairn went up. He hadn't thought the young fellow had it in him. By God! He must have had them all watched! In spite of his grievous perturbation the picture dealer actually chuckled. His kind likes an opponent worthy of its steel.

Well, now that he had solved the enigma—and how simple it was—the answer always IS simple when one has found it—he'd always said that—his path was clear. He must not hurry too much. He must think out his approaches. He must plan everything carefully.

Instead of taking the Tube he walked all the way back, slowly, though the evening, thoroughly discussing within himself every detail of the next moves.

He must discover in some way the details of North Merton House, or he must discover in what place there Delgairn was likely to have put it. There might be a choice of hiding-holes—there probably was more than one place. It might even not be in North Merton House at all—it might be with a devoted relative, or friend who was in the plot.

Then another point occurred to Bensington. If the thing was to be done in reasonable time, the more brains at work on it the better, and yet the more brains at work the greater chance of being betrayed.

He had two agents upon whom he could seriously rely for such research; he would put them to work, and they should approach North Merton after a fashion he would lay out for them.

There was Appleton, whom he had got from the

Regular Force at a very good salary, and who only six months ago had done that excellent piece of work in the case of the Russian Miniature. He had been well paid then, over and above his regular salary, and he would offer him a good bonus now. It would be *his* business to deal with the village and find out by that admirable approach what might have been done with the Masterpiece.

Then there was Ranford, not quite so able, but better at dealing with the domestic side of a house. He had taken service twice, and each time successfully. Indeed, he had played the footman so well that Henry Bensington would not have wondered if he had started his career as a footman before rising to the higher professional work in which he was now engaged.

Yes, that was it ! Ranford should get into the house, and Appleton should stay at the inn. Appleton should be a painter, putting up at the inn and Ranford somehow or other should take a place under the young Squire's roof. It could be done. What he would do at once was to get Appleton and Ranford round that very night and put the plan of campaign before them.

And so he did : Appleton, quiet, gentlemanly, a man with a nice accent and with a refined, reserved manner ; Ranford, smart, upright, well groomed—were given their orders and told the whole thing frankly and fully. They were given ample funds, for Henry Bensington knew by long experience how well he could trust them both. When he had dined at North Merton he had marked a handy man whom they sometimes put into livery when there were guests. They called him Joseph—though his real name was Joe. He must be bribed to have a relative fall ill suddenly, and to recommend Ranford for a few days to do the work in his place, Ranford being vouched for by the honest Joseph as a very old and well-known friend.

Appleton would take with him the same painter's kit as he had taken last time, when he had been working the affair in Huntingdonshire, and he would secure rooms at the Delgairn Arms the moment he heard from Ranford that *his* arrangements for taking the handy-man's place were completed. To avoid suspicion he had better get to the Delgairn Arms after Ranford was fairly installed in the big House.

It was a good plan of campaign. I can't remember whether I have said it before, but if I did I can say it again—it will do no one any harm. There *was* something Napoleonic about Henry Bensington, and, as you shall hear, he brought it off ; but like his great prototype the Corsican, not quite in the fashion he had intended.

CHAPTER XI

THERE are two men whom Charles Grant McCabe himself has called "the best picture-men in the continent of Europe." He said "continent." For without question in the British Isles Henry Bensington was the master of them all. These two men are M. Henri Caen of Paris and Mes Loisirs (a charming villa not far from Mentone), and Signor Carlo Alessandria, of anywhere you like, but generally of the Ritz Hotel in Madrid, the Ritz Hotel in Paris, the Ritz Hotel in London, the Ritz Hotel in New York, and the Ritz Hotel in Rome—(if there *is* a Ritz Hotel in Rome ; I forget).

M. Henri Caen is so prosperous that he has a *pied-à-terre* in England to which he retires when he does us the honour of visiting these shores. It is a cottage called The Thatch, at King's Worthy near Winchester. He makes no boast of it. He goes there to repose. His correspondence does not follow him.

Signor Alessandria also has a *pied-à-terre* in England ; it is a small house near Battle, called The Postern, the interior of which marvellously reproduces the effects of the XVth century. He makes no boast of it. He goes there to repose. His correspondence does not follow him.

It is a witness to the universality of genius that these two great men should have sprung from origins so utterly different. M. Henri Caen, though actually born in Vienna, where his parents happened to be residing at the time (and where, in his childhood, he acquired the inestimable advantage of speaking the German tongue), was brought up by his parents from the age of fifteen to the age of twenty-two in Paris. At that age of twenty-two he boldly launched out upon the career which made him, in the eyes of a thousand others beside Mr. McCabe, deservedly famous.

Signor Alessandria, upon the other hand, was born, of all places in the world, in Smyrna, where his parents happened to be residing at the time. His mother, and his father too, who were of doubtful origin, had German for a common language, so that the child had the inestimable advantage of acquiring that idiom in early youth. It was at the age of eighteen (what a proof of energy!) that from Malta, where his parents had for no less than three years become naturalized as British subjects, he set out upon that career which has made him in the eyes of a thousand others beside Mr. McCabe deservedly famous.

I have used the word "famous" of both these great men. Perhaps it is not justified. They are not famous to the general public. But their names are household words with the powerful groups which buy pictures, which sell them to the powerful groups which buy them again to hang upon their walls, or to have them bought again by friends in connection with the Government for permanent exhibition in the Great Galleries of Europe.

Both these gentlemen, M. Caen and Signor Alessandria, had appreciated, very early in the process, the rise of Bourrot. Each had heard a little too late of his declining health. Each had had communicated to him by a private agency the rather mortifying news that Henry Bensington had got in ahead of them. Neither of them landed upon these inviolate shores until the Masterpiece was already upon exhibition in Bond Street and Bourrot safely dead.

It was a pity—but so it was. M. Henri Caen had popped over and shown his passport at Folkestone upon the very day the Martin Rooms had opened to the public. Signor Alessandria had the misfortune to be delayed through some slight formality or other with *his* passport at Dover upon arrival by the morning boat an hour or two before M. Caen had triumphantly achieved Folkestone. Signor Alessandria therefore had hired a car. He might have saved his money, for he discovered (by the usual agency), upon reaching London that evening, that M. Caen was already there, and M. Caen had (by the usual agency) discovered that Signor Alessandria, who had telephoned for *his* rooms, was about to arrive. Happily they had chosen different hotels.

M. Caen, in whom the love of the beautiful mastered all other passions, had spent an hour early the next morning, while the Martin Rooms were still fairly empty, in thoroughly grasping the "*Ame Bourgeoise*." Signor Alessandria (his bad luck still pursuing him) did not get to the Martin Rooms till M. Caen had left them. He also spent, not quite an hour, but more than half an hour (so rapid is the Maltese mind) in noting and registering in his heart every effect, every detail, of the "*Ame Bourgeoise*."

So stood it with these two men, neither having met the other in London, each knowing that the other was there present, and each taking a certain precaution that he should not blunder into the other by any foolish accident. Indeed, Signor Alessandria, with the accustomed sensitiveness of the artistic soul, shut himself up in his rooms at the Ritz and had all his meals there, telephoning most of the day, and getting in sheafs and relays not only the daily papers, but sundry notes and advices. While M. Henri Caen, whether from fatigue or from a strange habit of isolation, remained apart from men in *his* rooms at the Paramount, telephoning much of the time, and receiving not a few advices by messenger as well.

Thus were both acquainted, within an hour the one of the other, of the interesting fact that the "*Ame Bourgeoise*" had been stolen. M. Henri Caen, stooping with difficulty—being of the figure affected by the French in middle life—pulled from his despatch box a large sheet of cartridge paper and began setting down headings to clear his mind upon what ought to be done.

Not so Signor Alessandria. He in *his* rooms, being of a lithe habit of body (and indeed younger than M. Henri Caen), could, had he chosen, have stooped with ease to pick anything out of any trunk of his. He preferred to .look out of the window and to think.

The result was the same. For each of these gentlemen, though their methods of staff work differed, was already possessed of the elements of the situation, and each of them enjoyed a brain rapid and acute: M. Henri Caen the logical, vivid but restrained brain of the Gaul, Signor Alessandria the logical, vivid, but restrained brain for which the Maltese are famous.

M. Henri Caen had no doubt about it. Henry Bensington was advertising. This theft-stunt in picture publicity is an old, stale thing—and a stern, ironic expression marked M. Henri Caen's face as he considered it. He had only to wait, and when the picture came back again it would be time enough to set to work.

Signor Alessandria, standing tall and erect before the big windows of his room in the Ritz, and gazing at the superb architecture of the new Devonshire House, had no doubt about it. It was a ridiculously stale trick, but Henry Bensington presumably knew his world and calculated it would go down. There was nothing to do but to wait till the picture came back and then to set to work.

It was thirty-six hours later, at five o'clock in the afternoon, that that gentleman who, in London, was in touch with M. Henri Caen about these things, telephoned to tell that prince of the picture world that the "*Ame Bourgeoise*" really *had* disappeared. He had no clue but Sir Henry Bensington's manner on getting back to his house from an expedition on foot—something rare with him. But there was no doubt something had gone wrong.

M. Caen spent about half an hour in co-ordinating, as they appeared, all the elements of the situation on the big sheet of cartridge paper which he had drawn up for his own guidance.

The "*Ame Bourgeoise*" had lain for years in the Château of North Merton. He had the railway station and all other relevant facts jotted down in his note-book weeks ago. It was Whitchell Station, three miles from the house. There were no cabs, but there was a taxi to be hired at the hotel opposite. The inn at North Merton was the Delgairn Arms—his Michelin gave it no telephone number. On that sheet of cartridge paper went down a further point concerning a conversation held by young Mr. Delgairn on the abominable sharp practice under which he was smarting—so thorough is organization in M. Caen's world. You and I, my dear reader, are ourself card indexed, bless us ! in this fashion, not only by the banks and by the police, but by all those of the modern world who have an interest in watching our affairs.

The Paramount has an A.B.C. in every room. There was a train for Whitchell at seven o'clock, arriving just before nine (abominably slow !). Yes, Whitchell was a small wayside station, and it was the first train available.

In spite of his French blood (or training ?) M. Henri Caen decided to do without dinner and subsist upon sandwiches on the way down. He risked getting a room at the Delgairn Arms, drove to Waterloo in good time—and so started his ball rolling.

It saddens me to tell you, my nice reader, that Signor Alessandria, with his usual abominable luck (fear nothing !) did not pick up his communications for a full twenty-four hours later, for it was not until M. Henri Caen had been casting about for contacts in the North Merton country during a full morning and half the afternoon of the next day, that Signor Alessandria was informed that the loss of the "*Ame Bourgeoise*" was genuine. On the other hand, *his* agent had given him much more precise details—which only shows that strategy is not only a function of time but also of information.

Signor Alessandria's intelligence department gave him plenty of elements for action : for it had tapped no less than three sources, each resident under Sir Henry Bensington's roof in various capacities, and at various prices. He was possessed of two essentials : (1) The envelope in which Delgairn's letter had come (with the North Merton postmark and its date), duly rescued from Bensington's waste-paper basket, and (2) What Bensington had muttered to himself at breakfast after the servant had shut the door—and then wisely opened it again for a minute, gently, to hear what might be heard.

Yes (Alessandria thought to himself as he turned again to that window and gazed once more with his hands in his pockets at the superb structure of the new Devonshire House), the Masterpiece was at North Merton House, or on its way there. His only trouble was the sure and certain faith that Sir Henry Bensington would have come to the same conclusion. Of M. Henri Caen, his arrival, his movements, he had heard nothing—as, indeed, had M. Henri Caen heard nothing of his. (And if you, wealthy reader, are puzzled by the blind spot from which these two great Captains suffered, let me tell you for your own private information that by so much as such men succeed in getting their information, by so much do they also succeed in obliterating their tracks.)

Signor Alessandria, having no cartridge paper, after the Gallic fashion (he did things in his head, after the more subtle fashion of the Maltese), had but to put the elements of the situation together in his own mind.

His conclusion was subtler and better than that of M. Caen. He did not reserve rooms at the Delgairn Arms—he wrote a letter to Harry Delgairn. (So Cæsar in his first campaigns !) There is a degree of genius which does these things. If you ask me, I would give the solid French brain of M. Henri Caen not more than sixty per cent. in the business of getting hold of stolen goods, but I would give Signor Alessandria something like close on eighty per cent. . . . not that I am for one moment belittling the Gallic genius as against the Italic. But on this occasion there could be no doubt that Signor Alessandria took the short cut—though he was (but without knowing it) twenty-four hours late.

His letter to Harry Delgairn was simple, stright-forward, and couched (if I may use the expression) in the Italian tongue. It would be of more effect. It would be read through with difficulty; or if, as was more likely, the young squire had no Tuscan, there would be certainly some gentleman in touch who could make it out with a dictionary. Signor Alessandria knew his England. All the letter said was that M. Alessandria had been an intimate friend of M. Bourrot, that he had heard how the Masterpiece had been sold, how sad it was that a picture painted for a particular house and so long in its right surroundings should have left them. Might he respectfully, on the plea of his deep affection for the dead genius, call upon the son of the man but for whose generosity that genius would never have played its great part in the world?

Signor Alessandria did not believe in pressing things. He was right. Yet on the second day he got his answer. Harry Delgairn had been touched profoundly (the scholarly Parson of North Merton had read the letter for him). Though he had an instinctive dislike of foreigners he sent a stiff note, saying that if Signor Alessandria did him the honour to call, he would be happy to receive him.

* * * * *

M. Caen read a guide-book during all his first breakfast at the Delgairn Arms, and occasionally asked questions in broken, but refined and quiet, English of the servant-girl. He wanted to know if the ruins of Rayton Abbey were open on week-days, whether one had to pay, exactly how far they were from the Inn, how much was left of them: on all of which the lively maiden answered at random, pleased to give information which she did not possess. M. Caen was delighted to find that she had an ingenuous mind and loved converse with her fellow-beings, especially with the enemy sex; even when it was alien and of a certain age. He received paternally her confidences. He learned with pleasure that she would never have come to such a dull place if it wasn't that her sister was parlourmaid at the big house, and that made it companion-like on days out and other times too; to all of which M. Caen nodded kindly.

"You see her?" said M. Caen, almost beginning to believe in a God in the presence of such startling luck. The Infant tossed her head and tilted her nose in the air.

"'Ardly!" she said. "If I'd a-known afore I wouldn't 'ave come . . . . Oh, 'e lets Millie go out all right, but he's that stuck up, 'e won't 'ave anyone in the house from the village. Can't so much as go there for a cup o' tea on my day out, if he 'ad 'is way." She tossed her head again. "'Tisn't 'is fault, perhaps, but 'e is that dull! Stodgy, *'e* is! Mutton-Face, I call 'im!"

"Your sister come to you—yes?"

"Oh, yes, she can come 'ere, so far as Master's concerned—he's a good man, is Master. But there again, that young chap Delgairn don't like 'is people in the village, 'e says." And she tossed her head for the third time.

"She do come, though?" persisted M. Caen.

"Oh, yes! She's a-coming to-morrow, for that matter. But she won't 'ave all the evening."

Now there are two ways of approaching any difficult task — such as theft, forgery, murder, or what-not — whatever it is that demands secrecy. One is the tentative, the other is the direct. The advantage of the tentative or groping-your-way method is that you can back out at the first sign of danger. The other, the direct, has the advantage that if you pull the thing off you pull it off at once and without delay. Where time is an essential, every master-mind will risk the second method, and Monsieur Henri Caen now risked it.

He knew how to make himself impressive through a certain slow diction and a lowering of the voice by four or five notes. He had done it before in this our Blessed Island, and he had found that it effaced the ridicule of his foreign accent and broken words. He tried it now, and with complete success.

"I am coming ere," he said, in that deeper manner, holding her with his eyes, "to do someting strange!"

He got up from his chair at the breakfast-table, shutting the guide-book, and still keeping his eyes upon

Courteous Insistence of a French Gentleman deeply versed in modern art with a Handmaiden of these Islands

the intrigued young lady, who was half alarmed, half attracted, by the mystery.

"I do not hide it, no! I tell you. There is in Monsieur Del Garne's great house a picture. A picture I come to see . . . . No," he added, seeing the look of fear come into the girl's face, "I do *not* come as a stealer. If I come to steal I tell you. I come only to look. It is not on de wall, it is idden away. I tell you why I would see it. I say it is not to steal it. I would see it for dis reason . . . . I did send the picture to Sir Del Garne's. It is a picture big like this."

Still keeping his eyes upon her, M. Caen pulled out a folded square of stiff paper from his pocket. He unfolded it, and held it before her. On it she saw something simple enough, its colours clear enough—it looked like a rigmarole, but there was no mistaking the one great glaring eye in a corner of the sketch. He gave it to her.

"It is little, I say, it is easily carried. It will be wrapped up. Yes? I know not. It is a French picture."

"Lor!" she said, gazing at the sketch. "It's a funny one!"

"It is a picture, French, I say to you. I did send it to Sir Del Garne's. It is French, like me. I also, I am French."

The maid brightened up a little and nodded. She had guessed right—he *was* French. It was a feather in her cap. She discovered that she was a clever puss!

And as she looked at the paper in her hand her judgment was confirmed in another fashion. She always had believed that foreigners were capable of anything!

"Sir Del Garne say he have it not. I say he have. If I say I know, and if he know I know, he pay. That picture I must see. Only see—and then I give him back."

He paused, and then discharged his big gun with reverberating effect. "There is much money for me to find the truth. I pay you, and her, your sister—one hundred pound."

Then he was silent, fixing her more steadily than ever with his eyes, and noting how her gaze staggered under their effect.

Before she could answer, he quietly pulled from his breast-pocket a bundle of twenty five-pound notes. "I give these," he said. "And I ask only to see and then I give back. Nothing more."

"I don't see what 'arm there'd be in it," murmured the tempted one. "It's not like stealing." She had hesitated—and was lost. He shook his head.

"There is no 'arm," he said. "And there is one 'undred pound." He pulled the wad of notes out again, then returned it to his pocket. "Is it not simple?" And he spread forth his hands, still keeping those eyes fixed upon her.

For her part, she turned abruptly from the room. But she took that garish sketch away with her. When she had gone, he sat down again and smiled to himself.

* * * * *

"There's no 'arm in it," she was pleading, as she talked to the young lady from the big house next day. "It isn't stealing. He only wants to look at it."

"It's not that," said Millie in a reverie. "That's all right. It's where it *is* that troubles me." (The parlourmaid was the realist of the two.) "There's only one place it could be, in a manner of speaking, and that's the lumber-room. It's not an 'ouse where they *could* 'ide anything." There was a little disdain in her voice as she said it.

"Well, there it is," answered her sister uneasily. "I wash my 'ands of your part."

"Oh, never mind me!" said Millie. She mused again. "There's a chest in the lumber-room, and two cupboards what they don't keep locked. It'll be 'ard if I can't find it. 'Ow much did you say?"

"'Arves!"

"'Arves it is," answered Millie loyally. They were not a quarrelling family. "Mind," she added, "you've got to have the notes in your 'and before I 'and the thing over—if I find it."

The handmaiden nodded, gave her sister M. Caen's coloured sketch for comparison. And yet another transaction was at an end.

* * * * *

Millie was in high good humour, and all the more in a mood for adventure. She was in good spirits because the young fellow who had come in the place of the handy man for a few nights had really made himself very charming. She only wished he was a Permanent. He had a way with him which was very superior to the Odd Man, and she wondered how two such different men could be such close friends.

But there! One did find that sometimes. There was her Uncle Joe, for instance, the chemist's man . . . you'd never take him to be father's brother. But then he 'ad studied, Uncle Joe had, and father had never done anything but booze. And how smart the young man did look in his livery, too. Not that she was taken in by clothes—she wasn't a girl of that sort. . . . He had such perfect manners. And then, he knew such a lot!

He knew, for instance, that the dark gentleman who had come to see Mr. Delgairn that afternoon was an Italian. Not that he knew the language, in a manner of speaking, but he knew the sort they were. He had met some of them before. . . . It was surprising how Mr. Delgairn had cottoned to him, seeing that he didn't like foreigners as a rule.

And so on! But she could not let her head run on like that, and she turned to the business in hand. It would be plenty of time to renew happy converse with the Temporary when things had been washed up, after dinner, and they were all sitting round downstairs to a bit of supper.

Millie's instinct was sound—and, after all, North Merton was the most simple of houses, even in the simple category of squires' houses. To put a thing out of the way nothing more complicated need be done than just to shove it up in the lumber-room, the big attic under the gable: and there was not much there. It was not like looking for a very small thing. She knew the size and the shape.

That very afternoon before it was dark Millie had gone through the cupboards. She had found nothing but a few coats, an old pair of climbing irons, some rusty skates, and half a dozen torn books. She had opened the big mouldy trunk. There was nothing in it but discarded rugs and things of that kind. She tried the large, low, heavy chest near the cobwebbed window. It was open, of course—nothing was ever locked up in that house. Right on the top of it were a palette, long disused, stiff brushes neglected for years, and half a dozen colour tubes, caked hard with time. Underneath these, folded round with a yellowing piece of newspaper which bore a date more than ten years old, she found a square parcel, and under it another square parcel of exactly the same size. She tried the one that came uppermost, she took off the coverings—and sure enough, she had found it!

A cloth protected it. She folded the cloth back and saw what she sought. There it was, unmistakable, just what the sketch, which she held in the fading daylight by the dirty window, had led her to expect to see. There was the Eye, and the ridiculous red and yellow bars, and the absurd fruit, all in their white frame.

Now that she had it, she felt, for the first time, afraid. She left the old papers all tumbled in the chest, wrapped the cloth quickly round the thing, and tiptoed out, down the creaking oak stairs. But really she had no need to take such precautions. She was only going about her ordinary duties. It was growing dusk, it was but a step through the gardens to the village. The bundle was small and easily hidden under her coat.

* * * * *

M. Caen had hired a car from the Delgairn Arms, and had spent an hour or two in the ruins of Rayton Abbey. He was interested in such things. When he came back he was exalted, pleased (but not excited) to find that the young lady whose acquaintance he had made had ready for him a certain small square parcel. Her sister had brought it, but could not wait. He nodded genially enough.

"It is already dark," he said, and shook his head. "I will have dinner. Then I see it. But it is no good till daylight None can judge oils in light artificial!" He shook his head again.

"But my sister can't wait, she 'as to get back at once," said his unhappy accomplice, hesitating.

"It is no good till I have dinner," repeated M. Caen firmly. "And even then it is no good. I wait till it is daylight. Give him to me, I put him in my room. To-morrow I look at him and make sure, and give him back. But wait. I must pay what I promise, is it not?" And he smiled charmingly, and handed over the wad of notes.

* * * * *

He had gone to dinner, and before sitting down had carelessly glanced for a moment to make certain (though he was certain already, dealing with such simple souls) that he had what he wanted. Even as he gave that glance, a Young Artist who had come to the hotel that afternoon, and who had been painting steadily as long as the daylight served, came into the dining-room and bowed to him.

They were to dine together, he presumed, and M. Caen courteously agreed.

They dined then, without undue haste, but M. Caen was worrying a little about the inn having no telephone. He even went so far as to say that an inn *ought* to have a telephone. The landlord came, apologetic, and said that there was no telephone nearer than the hotel opposite the station, three miles away; unless they went to ask leave for the one at the big house, and *he* would not like to do that.

No, said M. Caen, there was no need to do that. After the coffee he would take the car to the station, and telephone. Wait! How far had the landlord said it was? Three miles? Oh, he would walk—and the Young Artist courteously offered to accompany him.

They set out together on that little expedition. M. Caen, while his friend was outside getting his hat and coat, had the presence of mind to put the little canvas under the big cape into which he had struggled. Then the two set out through the fine night.

When they reached the little hotel opposite the

station M. Caen went in to telephone, and his young friend went to take a drink at the bar. M. Caen came out of the telephone box with an anxious look.

"It is grave!" he said, shaking his head. "Will you do something for me?"

"With the greatest of pleasure," said the young man. "Anything I can."

"Will you tell the patron at the hotel at North Merton that I have to go to-night, urgent, but re-come to-morrow—I re-come to-morrow, quick-early; eh?"

"I'm sorry you're going," said the artist, "but I'll certainly do it. I hope it's not bad news?"

"Oh, no, not that, but urgent," answered M. Caen, again with a worried look. "I vill go and find the train. There will be some train this night. . . ."

"Very well—good night," said the Young Artist, shaking the Frenchman warmly by the hand, and turning back to the bar.

M. Caen went out into the night, across the street to the station.

By one of those coincidences which fall thick in the lives of strategic men, there *was* a train for Winchester due some four minutes after M. Caen came into the station. He took a first-class ticket for that ancient city, and, as the train drew up, climbed into an empty carriage, somewhat burdened by the picture under his cape—but at any rate secure and with nothing to cloud his mind.

Just as the train jerked and gathered speed to draw

out of the station, the door of the carriage opened, and even as they left the lights of the platform the Young Artist jumped in.

He gave a hearty laugh, sank back into his corner, twinkled his eyes merrily at M. Caen, and said, "Only just caught *that!*"

And there they were, together again.

CHAPTER XII

As two generals, each of the highest genius, will blunder about in each other's neighbourhood, each with a suspicion that his rival is within range, so had those masters of commercial strategy, M. Caen and Signor Alessandria, lain in close proximity on that pleasant summer evening in North Merton; for even as M. Caen was negotiating at the Delgairn Arms for the temporary loan of the picture, Signor Alessandria was (after telephoning to his kind host Mr. Delgairn) motoring up the drive of North Merton House to pay his call upon the young squire. Even as Millie was turning over in her mind the great proposal, Signor Alessandria was having the door of that country house opened to him by the genial, the willing, Temporary Odd Man—who though an atheist (I am sorry to say) thanked God suddenly, and almost with a gasp, for the rapidity with which his plans were maturing.

Young Mr. Delgairn had that instinctive dislike of foreigners (except, of course, Germans, Americans, and perhaps Dutchmen—I ought also to add Swedes and Norwegians, and for that matter Danes) which is natural and inevitable in all healthy young men who have enjoyed the privileges of Public School education.

Whether of foreigners he most disliked Frenchmen, Italians, or Spaniards (let alone Belgians !) he could not have told you, for indeed he could not have distinguished between them.

Nevertheless, he received Signor Alessandria with courtesy, which ripened into something a little more genial when he discovered that this dark-haired and well-groomed man, with what he could not help admitting was a strong and decided cast of countenance—indeed, such a profile as he had met often enough in England—could talk English fluently. That was only natural in a Maltese devoted to the Empire, and, if not born within its boundaries, at any rate brought up in his teens under the Flag of Freedom.

But young Mr. Delgairn, having received his visitor's letter in Italian to begin with, was not prepared for such command of Shakespeare's (and his own) idiom—and he was pleased.

He hesitated a moment at first as to whether to offer the distinguished foreigner a drink, because he did not know what drinks the distinguished foreigner would drink. He was delighted to find that the distinguished foreigner was quite ready for a whisky and soda. More and more did young Mr. Delgairn admit within his heart that there was something to be said for exceptional foreigners like this—and all the while, as they drank together, the distinguished foreigner talked in so winning and yet so decisive a way about the landscape through which he had passed, the noble elms of the avenue, the

Young Mr. Delgairn, in spite of his instinctive dislike of foreigners, cannot resist the charm of Signor Alessandria

indescribable charm of the English countryside and of old English country houses such as this in which he found himself, that his host became almost friendly.

"May I show you one or two of the things I have here, Signor Alexander?" he said. "I expect you wanted to see something connected with Bourrot first, but unfortunately I have sold that picture, as you know." He tried to look grim, as he said this, but the word peevish would describe the mouth much better.

"Yes, yes!" said the Southerner with a sympathetic little gesture, almost imperceptible. "I know. . . . !"

"We have really nothing of Bourrot's that could interest you, I think—except a letter he once wrote to my father."

"Ah, indeed!" answered the other with flashing eye. "May I look at that?"

"Certainly, certainly. I have it ready for you here. I thought you would like to see it."

It was only the short note that had been left for Mr. Delgairn when the Masterpiece had been brought round to his hotel, but Signor Alessandria devoured it with adoring eyes. He sighed profoundly.

"Ah! How I envy you!" he said . . . "And how much more I envy you for living in such a house as this! We have nothing like it in our country. When I go back to my ancestral land, that of my cousin's in Emilia (Monte Acuto, you know)" (young Mr. Delgairn nodded as one gentleman to another. He did not know; but landed folk are a caste all over Europe). "When I go there," said the visitor, with a deprecating shrug of the shoulders, "what do I see? Fine marbles, formal gardens (my cousin is the head of the family), the cypresses, the fertile plains." He shook his head. "But not what I see here. There is a *comfort* about your English country house. How shall I express it . . . a *home* feeling."

Mr. Delgairn nodded. He had met a brother soul.

"Would you like to see over the house?" he asked.

Signor Alessandria was pleased that the suggestion should come first from his host, though he had certainly intended to bring it out himself if need be.

"Ah, what a privilege!"

They wandered about together; first they went to the stables and saw Rascal and West Wind, and then they patted Billy Boy on the head—who snapped at them. It wasn't worth while going down to the farm and scratching the pigs. Delgairn showed his distinguished guest the portrait by Reynolds of his Great-great-grandmother, the Constable, the old bit of parchment engrossed under Charles II., the billiard-room, the very oblong on the wall the unfaded paper of which showed where the Bourrot had hung (sideways); pretty well everything except the bedrooms.

Upstairs he showed him the gallery, and told him the stories of what had happened there in the Civil Wars. And Signor Alessandria listened with all his ears and soul. How absorbing! How unique!

"And what is up here?" he said lightly, as they

passed the only piece he had not seen (except the bedrooms)—a short rise of oaken stairs leading to some small dusty attic under the roof above.

"Oh, that's nothing," said Delgairn carelessly. "That's just a lumber-room. We needn't go up there. It's just where we put old trunks and broken pieces of furniture, and so on. . . . ."

And Signor Alessandria, with all the subtlety of an ancient civilization, registered young Mr. Delgairn's marked desire to avoid that room.

Said the picture dealer to himself (whether in German, Maltese or Smyrna Greek): "It's *there!*" But aloud he repeated, as he turned his back on the oak stairs to return to the ground floor, with his host: "All is so wonderful, so utterly *English!*"

And for half an hour more, as they sat over tea, he poured out so much knowledge of the things of England, and their contrast with the things of Italy, his dear native land (or rather, that of his ancestors; for Malta was his own dear island, he admitted—and that made him an Englishman, he hoped—with a smile), he poured out, I say, so fine a stream of sympathy and information that his host was ashamed to let him go.

"Really, Signor Alexander," he said, "I ought to have asked you before. But don't you think you could stop and dine? I can put you up."

"You are much too good!" said his guest with confused pleasure. "But I certainly cannot refuse you. I have my bag there in my car—I was driving back to

London to-night. There's nothing easier than to get it out and to go on to-morrow."

"That's excellent," said young Mr. Delgairn. He rang the bell and gave orders and had everything prepared for the comfort of the stranger; and excused himself for a moment while he hastily discussed the fare with the cook, and gave orders that the Temporary Odd Man should be in livery that night.

Signor Alessandria came down dressed with a care and yet an abandon which Delgairn recognized with admiration as worthy of the Blue Posts Club itself. He really had not known that Dagoes could rise to such things! And as the two sat down together, wine made the bond between them firmer still.

The reader, being a well-read woman, has heard of the fascination of the snake for the bird. I would not use the simile, for nothing shall make me compare Signor Alessandria to a snake, nor is there any bird that I can call to mind resembling young Mr. Delgairn—unless indeed it be the owl, boiled. The Maltese was thin but did not hiss. His host was no bright-eyed feathered songster, but a clean-bred, open-air young man of the best Public School type.

The reader will also, if she is acquainted with the best-worn of the classics, remember the Syrens, but I cannot compare Signor Alessandria to a Syren, and Mr. Delgairn was about as much like Ulysses as you are like a Chinese Mandarin. It is true that both Delgairn and Ulysses lived in the open air, but while one of them thought he was like a Greek God, the other did not. Let me rather say that the fascination exercised by Signor Alessandria was the fascination of a widely-travelled man of the world, seeming younger than he was (for his hair and moustache were properly darkened), over a young man who knew no more of the world than a pumpkin.

Nor did Signor Alessandria speak of Smyrna or of Malta, but rather of his ancestral estates in Emilia, of the heroism of his father (then a boy) and of his grandfather (then a dotard) under Garibaldi . . . . And so the long night wore on.

It was eleven o'clock before they took a nightcap each and parted firm friends with the prospect of a long morning before them on the next day, and the sincere regret of Delgairn to learn that his guest would have to leave in the forenoon.

* * * * *

At about twenty minutes to twelve all sound in the house seemed to have died down in the ears of Signor Alessandria—and they were acute ears. He had left his window open and his door ajar, and already twice, on tiptoe, sliding along the dark wall of the passage, he had listened at the head of the stairs; but all was absolutely still. There was no sound of footsteps above. There was no reflection of light upon the lawn. There was no moon.

He was no novice in the Smart Touch, the Get Away, although it only came occasionally in the way of business.

Indeed, it was three years since he had succeeded, with some difficulty, in the little affair at the Castello.

He thought he would give them an hour—and he gave them an hour.

It was a little before one o'clock (he had sat in the dark all the time) that he pulled from his pocket a tiny electric torch, neatly shaded with a small dark hood, put his hand over the slit where the light would show when he pressed the button, and tiptoed up to the long gallery.

As he went thus, stealthily, there followed him at a distance of about thirty feet, always round the next corner, the equally cautious figure of the Temporary Odd Man; but no longer in livery; dressed for the common world, with a soft felt hat crushed into his side-pocket, and a fat supply of bank-notes in his waistcoat pocket.

There was a momentary gleam as Signor Alessandria reconnoitred the oaken steps. Then it went out. The Temporary Odd Man slid into the darkness at the end of the gallery. In the lumber-room Signor Alessandria reconnoitred at ease. He was in no danger, he was out of ear-shot, and the little bulb gave him all the light he needed.

With a sure instinct he tried first the oak chest which stood plainly before him. He lifted the lid, and found, with an unpleasant shock, that certain papers within had already been disturbed. Someone had been there; something had been taken—and apparently that very day. There was thick dust on the outer part of the papers, while the inside was white and the cut in the string was clean. He moved those papers away with infinite precautions.

Below them he saw something which gave him another shock, but one of a more pleasurable kind. He saw a small oblong parcel, just the right size and shape. He made a cut with a penknife, with such precaution and silence that you could not have heard the rip two yards away, and he flashed the tiny ray on to what lay within the cover.

There was no mistaking it! It was a few square inches of that immortal, that unique canvas the "*Ame Bourgeoise*."

With agonized care, holding his breath to save all sound, and sliding away the loose papers about it with the gentleness of a trained surgeon, he drew forth the "*Ame Bourgeoise*," and got it under his coat.

Out went the little lamp, down the oak stairs went the cat-like feet—one would have sworn they were padded — down the main staircase, and then out by that French window which he had noted was not shuttered or bolted, and so out upon the lawn. It was pitch-dark, yet he still crept close to the wall.

Signor Alessandria had often had cause to bless the reign of law in England and the corresponding habits of casual ease. He had registered, when first he had come in, the open garage; he reached his car, and then bethought him of something so obvious one would have imagined he would have planned for it all beforehand—but he had not. A car starting at night is like the opening of machine-gun fire. And what would he do about the lodge gate ? There was nothing for it ; he must deal with that gate. It was a quarter of a mile off, and no one must hear him.

Keeping his loot carefully under his coat, he stole over the grass, avoiding the slight danger of the gravel, reached the gate, opened it with long, dexterous, sinuous gestures, and fastened the catch very slowly on to the stop to keep the gate wide back—the whole was done without a sound. There lay the exit, open for him to drive through at a charging speed.

He was back in the garage by the end of ten minutes ; he was in his seat at the driving wheel, his foot was ready on the self-starter. It was a warm night. There would be no trouble. He had a full tank. He would not switch on the light till he had taken the road.

All went well. At a greater pace than ever he had driven before in his life—and he was a fast driver—he had flashed through that short avenue, through the gate, and was racing down the lane for the Portsmouth Road.

Tiptoe on the luggage carrier, and clinging on to the back of the hood for dear life, crouched the Temporary Odd Man.

So went they through the night, by the aid of petrol, a great deal too quickly.

They could not have gone more than three miles when the first person who had turned in his sleep in

North Merton at the shattering noise of the engine starting (it was the chauffeur) was fully awake. The fugitive had gone perhaps eight miles when it occurred to that chauffeur to put on his clothes. Before the flying car had gone another ten that chauffeur was bawling for his master at the main door. Young Mr. Delgairn was with him, still half asleep and in pyjamas and dressing-gown, before Alessandria had gained a twenty-mile start. He was perhaps thirty miles away by the time the hunt was fully up, the lights turned on all over the house, and the telephone implored in vain to give some sign of life.

The further fortunes of that household we need not pursue. It was about an hour before the policeman came, another two before the house had been sufficiently searched and it had been made certain that nothing was missing. At last the early June dawn broke upon an insoluble problem. And by that time the roaring, racing, streaming Lancia was from eighty to ninety miles away upon its road, and smelling the stable, put on a new burst of speed.

The Temporary Odd Man had done wonders. But it had been a strain. Where his charioteer was taking him, he did not know. He prayed the adventure might soon end, for a Temporary Odd Man, even in mufti, hanging on by the luggage carrier and the hood of a racing Lancia car is a suspicious sight in broad daylight.

His heroism was rewarded. They were flashing

through the tumbled land of the eastern Weald before it could really be called day. By the time that a man could see the pattern of his coat in the dusk, the Lancia had swung round a sharp turning, down a short by-road, up a shorter drive, and stopped with a grinding of brakes before a quite little secluded cottage; just what a man engaged in the purchase and sale of the Beautiful might choose. Signor Alessandria, stretching his lanky body and throwing up his arms with the relief from strain, had reached his home.

The Temporary Odd Man crouched low. He had some dread that the Lancia would be backed against the wall of the garage; he risked it, and was saved by a couple of inches. He saw his involuntary conductor stoop into the back part of the car to take out the Masterpiece, raise his upper body, pull a key from his pocket, and begin walking towards the cottage door. It was now full daylight.

The Temporary Odd Man kept close behind his involuntary host. When that host had one hand engaged with the key, the other grasping the parcel which held the picture in its frame, the Temporary Odd Man put a hand suddenly on his shoulder, and said, audibly but not too loud:

"One word, and you're done!"

Signor Alessandria instinctively let go the key in the lock, and moved a hand towards a certain pocket. That hand was caught by the Temporary Odd Man.

"Far better not!" he said.

They looked in each others eyes.

"Let me in with you, and we'll talk it over. I think you'll find we can do business. I may as well tell you we know all about it."

Who "we" might be the ingenuous native of Smyrna, inhabitant of Malta, citizen of the Empire, guest of Great Britain, associate of the Landed Gentry, firm and resolute driver of nocturnal racing cars, knew not. But in a flash he decided that the advice was sound. Business, of whatever kind, was business, and revolver shots attract attention.

He turned the key, swung the door open, motioned the Temporary Odd Man to enter before him, in a flash whipped out his Browning, and followed his guest, in that charming attitude, I will not say of suspicion, but of proper caution which is justified in an armed man against him whom he supposes to be unarmed. The Temporary Odd Man, I need hardly assure you, had his left hand loosely engaged in his coat-pocket, where it toyed with another little instrument of the same sort. For to know how to shoot from the pocket is the first element in a training for The Active Life.

* * * * *

It was while young Mr. Delgairn had been enjoying those moments (alas! too brief) of brilliant conversation with Signor Alessandria at his own table that the Young Artist, who had jumped into the carriage at Whitchell Station, was saying so genially to M. Caen, "Only just got it!" It was while young Mr. Delgairn and Signor Alessandria were taking their first sip of port that M. Caen was deciding, with the rapidity demanded by the occasion, how that occasion should be met. While he yet turned the problem over in his mind his companion met him half-way.

"Well, M. Caen," he said, " — you'll excuse me using your name ? It's deservedly famous !—so we're travelling together ? "

M. Caen made no reply.

"That's as it should be," said the Young Artist, crossing his legs and leaning back comfortably. "I don't often go first, I can't afford it ; but when I saw you taking a first class ticket, I thought it would be a pity to miss your company. We're all going the same way home."

Still M. Caen was silent. The Young Artist went on, in the most self-possessed way in the world.

"I say," he said, "can you put me up ? "

M. Caen then at last spoke, slowly, and with pauses between each word.

"I—do—not—know—you," he said.

"No ? I know you don't. But, upon my soul, I don't know where I can get put up for the night. We're both getting out at Winchester, it'll be very late, and I've got to go up to town early to-morrow morning. It's quite on the cards that they won't open to me at the inn—you see, I've got no luggage."

Again M. Caen was silent. He was thinking desperately. He remembered stories of gentlemen trapped in railway trains who had cut the knot by pushing their trapper out of the door. But there was quite twenty years between him and the genial Young Artist; besides which, England is a crowded country, and heavily over-policed. He bent forward and said hoarsely, in the same slow fashion:

"What—is—it—that—you—want?"

"I've told you," said the Young Artist, with increasing *bonhomie*. "I want you to put me up for the night. Then to-morrow we can both go up to town together, eh? You'll bring that with you," he added, nodding sideways towards the parcel which poor M. Caen had risked so much to obtain. "And we'll both go off to old Harry Bensington. He's a friend o' mine."

M. Caen sat back, keeping his eyes fixed firmly upon this unexpected captor.

"It's all quite clear," went on his companion. "We know all about it. You go to Bensington, as I say--it's much the best way out of it. Then I can pretty well promise you there'll be no prosecution. If you kick there *will* be. While you were off and I was in the pub I left a message, so that they could trace you anyhow. Now be a sensible fellow, and do as I tell you."

M. Caen rapidly recapitulated the various Ways Out. He found each of them locked and barred. Violence was out of the question. Escape was out of the question—there was no doubt who could run the faster. Appeal to the public force was out of the question—the chances were that this fellow had proofs on him, and could turn the tables: he might even be from the Yard. Anyhow, M. Caen himself was on the wrong side of the criminal law, and he knew it. He was in possession of stolen goods.

"Come now?" said the Young Artist. And M. Caen answered: "Very well!" Not another word was exchanged.

At Winchester they got out. M. Caen, holding his precious parcel convulsively, waddled with the well-directed steps of a man who knows the map at such an hour to the one garage where they would always serve him, day or night. He motioned to his new-found friend to get in first, and together they drove the short miles.

In the pleasant little cottage in King's Worthy at which they drew up M. Caen suggested bed for the Young Artist, and the Young Artist suggested bed for M. Caen. Each desired the custody, or at any rate the permanent company, of the Masterpiece.

It ended by their sitting up in chairs opposite each other throughout the short remaining darkness. Twice poor M. Caen nearly dropped asleep, and from his heart the other pitied the older man; but duty was duty and a commission was a commission—it looked like a large one!

M. Caen never really dropped off, and he was exhausted when, towards seven o'clock, they heard the only and aged servant clumping downstairs. The owner of the house ordered coffee, and politely asked his guest what he would like to have, as he himself followed the continental custom and only took a little bread and coffee. The Young Artist was quite agreeable and equally polite: he would take whatever M. Caen was good enough to offer. After the coffee, might he telephone? It would hardly be worth while before nine o'clock, but might he telephone at nine? M. Caen had a telephone, he presumed? Yes, M. Caen assented in an iron tone, unemphasized. The younger man might telephone at nine o'clock.

Therefore it was that at 8.45 o'clock sharp the Young Artist was on to the rooms in King Street. He knew Bensington's habits. Sir Henry must not be disturbed before nine. The message could be left. The Secretary always came in at exactly half-past eight. The message was the one agreed upon, with the blanks filled in. "Tell Sir Henry that what he was expecting has been obtained. Tell him I am here with M. Caen, at King's Worthy. He and I will come up together . . ." To Caen: "Have you got an A.B.C.?"

The victim reached to the shelf and handed his gaoler the local time table. The man at the telephone glanced at it rapidly. Then he said to the telephone:

"Let me see . . . yes, we'll be up at Waterloo by two and with you before half-past. . . . Does that suit you?" he added, turning to M. Caen over his shoulder. And M. Caen silently nodded.

* * * * *

At the other end of the wire, the Secretary had barely

hung up the receiver when there was another sharp ring. He took it up.

" Please give Sir Henry the following agreed message " (the Secretary took up his pencil) : " What he is looking for has been obtained. I have it here at Battle, and am coming up with it, and Signor Alessandria, reaching your office just before four to-day."

Before the bewildered Secretary could make a comment upon so astonishing a discrepancy the wire went dead again, and there was no number with which he could communicate.

CHAPTER XIII

When Sir Henry Bensington came into his room at his exact and punctual hour, and prepared to go through his correspondence, his secretary, that invaluable coadjutor put first before him the two telephone messages. He rightly judged that they would have to be dealt with at once.

The great Dealer took up the first and read it rapidly with a changing and rising expression.

"Ah!" he said in real relief and content. "Good work! I've always suspected that fellow Caen. But as for the tracking of him, I've never known anything much smarter!" He looked again at the message. "They'll be here by half-past two. Well, that gives me time to turn round. I think I know what I shall do. Good business, isn't it?" said he, looking at the younger man and speaking with a rare familiarity.

"Yes, sir," said the secretary obediently. "But . . . there's a second message, sir, I think . . . would you like to look at it before you turn to the letters."

Henry Bensington picked it up. "I thought it was a duplicate," he said. Then his brow puckered, he drew his under lip between his teeth, read the first message again, read the second again; and said angrily: "Look here—what's this?"

"It's just as I received them, sir," said the other, with proper self-respect. "I think you can rely on me. . . ."

"Oh, yes, yes, yes" (half angrily). "I'm not blaming *you*. That'd be silly. Of course, I'm not blaming you. But" (exploding) "damn it all, man! It doesn't make sense! Did you hear the voices?"

"Quite plainly, sir."

"You recognized them?"

"Oh, yes, sir. Appleton first, Ranford the second."

Bensington frowned more deeply, and turned his mind inward. He could make nothing of it. The picture had been discovered, in the lair of that old rascal Caen, at King's Worthy. Yes, he remembered that he had on his card-index that address of King's Worthy for Caen's cottage in England, where he lived under the name by which he chose to go in that locality, very retired, very well chosen for repose.

"Then, what on earth was this message from Rye?"

He turned to it again, and saw that in his first confusion he had missed the essential name—Alessandria.

He looked quickly up at his secretary.

"Would you go to my card-index cabinet—here are the two keys" (handing them)—"and look up if we have any note of Signor Alessandria's movements. Has he taken any place near Battle?"

The secretary came back. "It must have been recent, sir. We have posted him up to less than a month ago, with all the reports from Lyons and Rouen, and his interview with the Curator of the Museum there and the false passport. There's nothing about Battle."

"Well, it's at Battle they've got him, so it's at Battle that he is . . ". and again Bensington frowned. . . . "It's incredible," he added. "Unless one of them's gone mad. They each knew the picture well enough . . . and they're both trained men." He looked again at the second message. "Humph! A little after *four?* Reach me the A.B.C., if you please. Yes, that's it. He's made allowances for the probable delay, and he's coming up by train. Well, I suppose I shall see clearer when the time comes—but it's all Greek to me now."

* * * * *

At King's Worthy the elderly and exhausted M. Caen, short of a night's sleep, went off with his captor in the little hired car to Winchester station. But on one thing he had insisted. He was held on a leash . . . the Young Artist had no authority . . . and if anyone touched the picture save himself he would struggle, he would make it an assault and summon aid.

He was willing to go quietly and to interview Bensington. But the Masterpiece was there, and it was an asset, and he was not going to let it go.

He took the precaution of slipping the end of the string which bound it through a buttonhole in his coat, and knotting it; then he tucked the parcel under his arm, and held it firmly there all the way up to town and in the cab all the way to Bensington's office in King Street.

Thereinto was he ushered, just before the hour which the Young Artist had named in his telephone message —half-past two o'clock. The Young Artist, with a courtesy worthy of a better cause, with the chivalric honour of an older world, allowed the French picture-dealer to enter Bensington's office and presence alone. He softly shut the door, and went round himself to another compartment by a passage at the back—which other compartment was separated by a curtain only from the study where the interview was taking place.

M. Caen and Henry Bensington faced each other. Caen with the Picture in its wrapping still under his arm. Bensington with hands in coat-pockets, resolute and ready.

They were alone—save, of course, for Mr. Appleton behind the curtain.

Henry Bensington spoke in German — happily a common medium for both:

"Well, M. Caen? Will you noble like hand over my property which you in your hold have there?"

It was the turn of M. Caen to speak. He spoke gently, and with perfect restraint, as behoved his Gallic blood: while the fact that his protest also was in German lent it an added depth.

"And what if your so-direct proposal I cannot acceptably entertain?" said he.

"Then it is simple," answered Henry Bensington,

Mossou Caen gently puts the alternative

with decision. "I prosecute you for the receiving of stolen goods, knowing them to be stolen. You are a well-known picture dealer, no one will believe that you were not acquainted with Bourrot's great work. It is prison, you know. Take it or leave it." He had also some acquaintance with the past of M. Caen.

M. Caen neither took it nor left it—he stood silent, considering the matter in his mind very carefully.

He also was in the trade; he also knew very well what was meant by these periodical "thefts" of pictures; he also knew a great deal about Henry Bensington's earlier life. But then he knew also a good deal about the English judicial system, about the powers of money in our society, about the advantages of living in England after being born in Cologne, compared with living in France after being born in Vienna. He turned the whole thing over in his admirably sane judgment, and he came to his conclusion.

"I will your conditions accept," he said.

Sir Henry Bensington looked down at the table and at his own hands laid thereon. He asked to see the back of the canvas. M. Caen held it up. Bensington said gently:

"M. Caen, I do not wish unknightly like to deal hardly with you. I want to tell you two things. First, the picture you have brought back is not the original. It is a replica, and a rather bad one. On the original, which I have had the misfortune to lose by theft, but which I hope to recover, I painted, upon the back of the frame, a circle, very prominent and unmistakable. I did it with my own hand. I know how often these valuable things are reproduced, and I wished to safeguard myself. Excuse me if I do not tell you what colour it was. Now, nothing of that sort has been scraped from the picture you brought me; even if it were a good copy, which it is not, it does not bear the faintest traces of this mark, and the absence of this mark would be enough to condemn it. That is the first thing I have to tell you."

M. Caen remained silent, and his features betrayed neither surprise nor mortification.

"The next thing I have to tell you is this. I am not going to make you lose by a transaction which is, after all, more or less in our way of our common business. I trust I have more professional feeling than to do so. Though what you have brought back to me is worthless, I recognize that you have been put to some expense in tracking it down—we all have these expenses—and I shall be happy to hand you, here and now, when you give me the canvas, a cheque to order for £500—only, of course, I must ask you for a receipt in due form."

M. Caen, whose judgment was rapid as well as sound and profound, replied without hesitation.

"The receipt. Have you prepared it for me in due form?"

For answer Henry Bensington pulled a long stamped slip of paper out of his pocket, with the cheque attached to it by a pin; and M. Caen duly signed: writing the word "Caen" all by itself, like an English peer or a French Bourgeois (which he was) accompanied by remarkable little twirls and flourishes after the fashion of the French Bourgeois rather than of the English peer (which he was not). It was a receipt for £500 "for researches undertaken in tracking the missing Masterpiece of Bourrot, which researches had unfortunately proved fruitless."

"Thank you!" said Sir Henry, putting the paper back into his pocket. Like the honest Englishman he was, he extended his hand. I am sorry to say that M. Caen only tapped that hand gently with the nails of two fingers and shuffled off, smiling a very unplesaant smile.

But just as he was going through the door, Sir Henry Bensington put up his hand and called him back.

"One moment, M. Caen," he said politely.

The gentleman with whom M. Caen was only too well acquainted, from a journey they had taken together in the train, came in from the opposite side of the room.

"You heard all that passed?" said Sir Henry quietly.

"Yes, sir. It's all down here in the German in my notes."

"Right!" said Sir Henry, nodding.

And M. Caen again went out.

* * * * *

Not long after M. Caen had left the Presence with bowed head, one of the very powerful engines of the Southern Railway (formerly the property of the South

Eastern) drew up, not more than half an hour late, into its London terminus—nor had there been from Battle more than three changes.

Signor Alessandria had indeed suggested to the Temporary Odd Man that they should go up (as it was a very fine morning) by car, pointing out that it would be much more convenient. The Temporary Odd Man had pointed out in his turn that the train was a great deal more comfortable.

Signor Alessandria regretted this conflict of judgment, for his acute and rapid Italic mind had grasped the possibility of a slight accident, in which, even if the Temporary Odd Man were to suffer somewhat, he himself could go forward to summon aid. Signor Alessandria was a skilful driver; and the misfortune of the Temporary Odd Man, seated on the near side, might be managed at any convenient corner.

Much the same train of thought had passed through the Mind of the Temporary Odd Man, despite its lack of Italic rapidity. He preferred the train.

Signor Alessandria was not his own master; he did not plead further; he accepted the decision. And he was glad to note that the Temporary Odd Man made no bones about the actual handling of the canvas. Signor Alessandria kept the little frame in its wrapping close behind him, between his back and the cushion, all the way up to town.

They were shown into Sir Henry Bensington's room together, but the master of the place motioned to the

Temporary Odd Man that he should withdraw—which he did, going round by the passage and getting behind that curtain in the opposite wall which had so recently concealed his colleague.

Henry Bensington sank back in his chair and sighed. He was not often fatigued, but this twin business, this double performance, he found a little exhausting. However, it had to be gone through. Since M. Caen had departed there had been a good half hour by the schedule. He had drunk a glass of sherry and taken a biscuit, smoked a cigarette, and was refreshed.

When in due course Signor Alessandria was thus ushered in, with that obsequiousness which his truly distinguished appearance had commanded from the well-trained domestic, Sir Henry bowed to his colleague, his fellow-professional, his brother expert, his co-lover of pictorial beauty, his associate in the worship of Apollo, and spoke thus :

" I do not desire to detain you, Signor Alessandria—perhaps we may as well get to business at once."

The well-groomed guest made no sign of understanding. He answered in the Italian tongue that he was not possessed of the English idiom. Luckily he had the inestimable advantage of having learnt German in youth. That tongue being equally familiar to Sir Henry, he, in the virile accents of the Teutonic forests, told Signor Alessandria without reserve what he thought of him. He repeated the remarks in French, and (what was really astonishing—but Sir Henry actually possessed a little Maltese) in Maltese. Perhaps he would have gone on in the Greek of Smyrna, but Signor Alessandria replied in German, without irritation, but also without the least subservience. He knew what Sir Henry Bensington demanded of him—he demanded the "*Ame Bourgeoise*," which he, the Signor, had there on a chair beside him. But Signor Alessandria knew the value of that picture, which he had acquired with very great difficulty. He was not prepared to let it go, save, of course, after negotiation.

"Negotiation even of the simple between market-men, boorish cow-driver sort there will not be," answered the English baronet—with a mastery of the idiom he was using!

Signor Alessandria lifted his head. With a well-restrained decision, he put a hand behind his back, leant his elbow on the table, and politely inquired in staccato accents, unusual to those who take advantage of their German knowledge, what would happen to him if he refused?

Sir Henry Bensington pointed out the nature of the situation: the fact that the picture had been stolen, and that however Signor Alessandria might have obtained it, he remained either a receiver of stolen goods or, now that the facts had been put before him, a detainer of them. Sir Henry briefly recapitulated sundry recent cases in the Courts showing what happened to people who place themselves in this false situation.

Signor Alessandria hesitated, but he was still game.

Signor Alessandria puts the alternative with verve

Sir Henry Bensington brought up his reserves, in another order from that in which he had used them against his late French opponent.

"Further, I may tell you," he said, "that your labour has been thrown away. The picture you have is not the original. Pray hold it up for me to see. Yes. It is a copy, and a very bad copy. But even if it were the best of copies, I can prove it to be not the original. Before I let the original go I painted a small but very conspicuous cross on the back of the canvas. I know how often these things are copied, and I did it with my own hand. I will not tell you the colour. Will you kindly turn the frame round and let me see the back? It is as I say. There is no sign whatever of any obliteration upon yours. That cross was never there. And to that cross I have witnesses." He rang a bell, and the gentleman who had taken that so rapid nightly drive with Signor Alessandria came from behind the curtain.

"You remember my marking the original?" said Sir Henry.

"Certainly, sir. It was with a cross in v . . ."

Signor Alessandria pricked up his ears—which, though not actually pointed, were acute. He would have given his eyes to hear whether the missing word was Vermilion or Veridium; but an angry glance from Sir Henry had checked his subordinate: angry, I say, though there was mixed in that glance not a little admiration for Ranford's quickness in adding detail to an imaginative composition.

Signor Alessandria still hesitated. Sir Henry set forth

the affair in a very few words. He put his clenched hand down on the table, knuckles outwards and leaned towards the foreigner.

"You have the choice between two things," he said. "An immediate prosecution, for which this gentleman" (he turned to his agent) "can bear sufficient witness, and on which I have collected (I may tell you) a mass of corroborative detail: an immediate prosecution for the reception of stolen goods—I may add that I should act with Mr. Delgairn in this matter; or" (and here he changed his tone) "an offer I am prepared to make you. As against a formal receipt which I have here with me, I will give you an open cheque for £500. Now, sir," he said, sitting down abruptly and gazing strongly at the still suave, still well-controlled figure before him, "there's your choice! Prison, or £500. I am speaking in English this time, and you can well understand me."

Signor Alessandria replied in German. He said simply that he could not follow what was being said, but he supposed that an offer was being made for the picture, which he had recovered, and for his services in the recovery of it. He would be happy to accept.

Henry Bensington produced a receipt identical in form with that which M. Caen had signed a short time before. Signor Alessandria read it carefully.

"It is in English," said Sir Henry ironically. "Can you read it?"

Signor Alessandria answered in German, that though he could not speak the language of Galsworthy, he could read it. And taking from his waistcoat pocket a very elegant gold fountain-pen he signed the two words "Carlo Alessandria," and added without a blush the five further words, "di Monte Acuto d'Emilia." Then he took the cheque, bowed very low, and went out with a vigorous dignity which did honour to the blood of the Scipios, the Catos, and all the rest of them: but still more to the Monte Acutos d'Emilia.

CHAPTER XIV

HENRY BENSINGTON had found through a long and successful business career that when the mind was bewildered by some apparently insoluble problem the very best course was to dismiss it for some hours, and return to it as fresh as need be, with the tonic of friendship and varied conversation in between.

He rang up one of his six clubs where he could best depend on good company, was delighted to hear the names of three at least who were already present. He motored there for a long, comfortable and very lively dinner, meeting for the first time, and getting interested in the conversation of a man who was going to the Arctic.

The later hours he deliberately passed in further company, at Peggy Ralton's, the house with which he was perhaps most intimate in all London ; he waited on deliberately, keeping his mind away from the incredible situation which awaited him when he should return. But even during the few minutes in his motor between that hospitable house and the familiar rooms where he proposed to meditate upon his next move the riddle returned to him with full force.

He saw, as it were, in the darkness before him, those

two identical "*Ames Bourgeoises*," and the vivid mental image gave him a shudder. It was well past midnight when he sent the motor away, bolted the outer door, went up the narrow steps, switched on the lights in his study, went into the back room to the safe, brought out the two pictures, one in either hand (handling each as carefully as though it were the real one), and then, returning to his study, locked the two doors of that room, propped the pictures up before him, side by side, drew up his chair, and sought inspiration from the very presence of that baffling duality.

* * * * *

For the first full hour of the night Henry Bensington sat with arms on the table, leaning forward and attempting to solve the insoluble: What was this nightmare? What were these monstrous twins? Which was the original? Which the incredible duplicate? And why? Then again—leaving that—what was he to do?

If he preserved both, keeping one secret and proclaming the other as the recovered treasure, the suppressed one might come out by accident in a second theft—and then the value of the first was destroyed.

The obvious course was to destroy one and sell the other. But what if he destroyed that one which some later evidence should prove to be the original? No . . . he must neither suppress nor destroy!

But then . . . what was to be done?

He stared at those twin canvases hour after hour

Sir Henry Bensington, Master of Great Affairs, wrestling with a mighty problem through the watches of the night

through the darkness. They possessed him. He fell into that sort of trance which comes of long concentration, and which all those know who have faced a mighty and single problem by night and in complete isolation. It is an abnormal state wherein external perception ceases and the sense of time is cut off. Under that influence the reason also seems paralysed. The two elements of the dilemma stand stark like iron sphinxes, not even repetitive: permanent, dominating, changeless.

No release is conceivable. Yet all the while the solution approaches by its own unseen avenues, and it is at the end of such vigils that sudden discoveries come. Two o'clock struck, and three, and four, from the gilt Empire clock under its glass case. He never heard the sound. What broke the bonds was a streak of grey at the shutter-join. It was dawn—and Henry Bensington lifted his head with a shock to the real world. Fatigue came rushing upon him, and with it an immediate, immense necessity for sleep. He rose and staggered to his room, tore off his clothes and fell into a deathly torpor—but in the few seconds between his extinction of the light and nothingness revelation had arrived. It came to him as from without; something not then to be examined by the exhausted soul, but impressed profoundly: and when he abruptly woke, staring at the late morning, the plan stood clear before him, and he had only to act.

* * * * *

There stands in a by-street of Chelsea a small and

curious shop, dingy, crammed with a mass of salvage from chance sales, a collection which seems always much the same, now one oddment going, now another added—but rarely. Therein, under the poor light of its one grimy bow-window of diverse small rounded panes, shuffles and squeezes between the dusty what-nots, the files of dustier books upon the floor, the jaded mirrors and grandfather clocks, the sere, bent figure of old Mr. Gabriel. The neighbours cannot remember a time when he was not there, and they guess, rightly, he has some private means sufficing his very meagre life—for certainly his business would never keep him. He is a pensioner of Sir Henry's, serviceable and tightly held ; and to his pension are added good little commissions for any occasional find, but also regular reminders of his duty and of the consequences of failure. But there is now little need for such checks. Habit and the indifference of age have made Mr. Gabriel a faithful agent, and he will deal with large matters as with small at his master's bidding most punctually : he has become as reliable as a thing mechanical. To him, a little before noon on the morning when Henry Bensington awoke from coma, came, by hand, a sealed message summoning him at once to the famous rooms in King Street, Mayfair : a taxi waited.

Meanwhile, in those famous rooms, what Henry Bensington was doing was this :—

He bolted the outer door of the private study. He laid the two, small twin canvases face downwards on the green baize of the central table, he lit a candle, took out his tie-pin and reddened the point in its flame. Then, with that fine instrument he rapidly burnt one most minute hole into the top left-hand corner of one frame back, another in the top right-hand corner of the other. The first canvas he took rapidly off to the safe and locked it in. The second he turned right way up on the table and awaited his servant.

He had not long to wait. Twelve had but just struck when there came a knock at the study door. Bensington opened it himself, and himself bolted it behind old Mr. Gabriel, who shuffled in, alone, as he had been bidden to be in the message, and twisting his thin, clasped fingers, awaiting orders.

The orders were clear and brief. They involved a sum of money—but Mr. Gabriel was used to that. He had passed on many such—no one of them quite so large, but in the aggregate and over many years, enormous—and his tiny commissions, hoarded without purpose over so many years, were his absorbing interest. He heard what his commission was to be in this case, and he was more than content. He knew it would be paid at the moment of delivery. And the details of delivery were made clear. He need not hurry. It might be days before the client would come (the name was given), but once the transaction was finished there would be need for promptitude. The money, when it was taken by him, was to be paid within the hour by hand, not post, at King Street. Mr. Gabriel would then have his little commission in cash, and all would be in order.

Mr. Gabriel would approach the usual two wastrels about town, Young Belter and Stocky Grahame, who were always ready to earn an odd fiver. Here was the money, and also cash for that day's expenses.

With that Henry Bensington covered the canvas before him with a thickness of good cardboard and a large blanket cloth, made up all into a parcel of brown paper, tied it and handed it over. Mr. Gabriel took it to the cab waiting outside and so to Chelsea. Thus, and privately, are the main matters of this world often arranged.

The bait was set, and there was nothing more to be done but to wait.

* * * * *

That same evening, that fine warm evening of June, just after seven, the two wastrels paced up and down Little Rodney Street behind the Plantagenet Hotel. The tall one, Young Belter, was still in a morning coat. He was to dine later and to dress in his rooms. He made a fine young figure of a man with crisp close hair and strong features, decided eyes and a pleasant voice.

The short one, Stocky Grahame, was perhaps ten years older, less individual (as they used to say) but with a worldly look and quietly assured. He was dressed for dinner—and to the nines.

Each had upon him, with much lesser cash, a nice new

five-pound note which had lately been in Mr. Gabriel's hands and before that in Sir Henry Bensington's.

It was not the first time they had forgathered in that quiet backwater. It would not be the last; for many upon whom they operated stayed at the Plantagenet when they came to London, and there was a private door in Little Rodney Street very convenient for immediate entry when all details were settled and a plan ripe for execution.

"You're sure the Duke will be there?" asked stocky White Waistcoat and Butterfly Tie, looking up to his tall young companion.

"Absolutely," answered tall young Morning Coat. "I asked Percy in the office not five minutes ago. Besides which, he's always in the bar getting a cocktail on the tick. Never knew him miss a day since he came over—and he's expecting me."

They compared watches.

"Barge into us at twenty to eight *exact*, in the lounge. We'll be off to dress, both of us, after that, he and I."

"You're not dining with him?"

"No . . . it's better to let it sink in."

"All right. Twenty to eight. In the lounge." And White Waistcoat went off to pass the time at Buffles, while Morning Coat passed through the private door into the Plantagenet.

In the Bar, as fate and right demanded, he found the Duke of Emonsillado slowly sucking a Sudden Glory through two straws. He had known the young man off and on for two years and met him at random when he came over to London, and they had made an appointment by telephone that afternoon to meet and have a drink and swop news. Morning Coat had rung him up at five.

His Grace received him warmly, for he liked the company. It put him wise—Morning Coat knew so much about London.

There was less starch than ever about the Grandee of Castile and Aragon that evening. He was in the mood called Hail-Fellow, and he asked the young man what was his. A name was given it, and the two took ten minutes or a quarter of an hour to manage the first two cocktails in their big leather chairs side by side. Hardham heard lots of entertaining things: about the police raid at Crippins and why another magistrate tried the case and how Biddy Barry gave her old aunt's name and how the Home Secretary got away over the tiles. At last, at the third cocktail, Morning Coat added, after a short silence:

"I forget if you care about pictures?"

"Naw," answered El Duque. "Not since them Talkies."

"I mean paintings."

"Aw! . . . . Why?"

Morning Coat leant over and said in a lower tone:

"*Someone's found Harry Bensington's Bourrot.*"

The Duke showed little interest. Morning Coat continued:

"You heard about the stealing?"

"Yep"—still with no enthusiasm.

"Well," and here Morning Coat sank his voice to a murmur and looked round to make sure no one would hear. "Harry Bensington won't see it again! First thing he'll know it'll be safe away, and it won't come out till everything's blown over. Guess who's got it?"

His Grace shook his head, a trifle bored.

"Old Gabriel! Know old Gabriel's cache?"

"Naw."

Morning Coat precisely described the position, street and number of the little dingy shop in Chelsea; the bow-window, the elderly grey figure of the man himself, all the bag of tricks; even the early hour at which the place opened of a morning . . . . Then, politely deferring to his host's evident boredom, he went on to discuss the chances of Henry the Second at Goodwood and after that the Tillington divorce, and after that the Steyning case . . .

But all the while he was aware of the clock—and at twenty-two minutes to eight he rose and led the older man towards the lounge, saying he must be off to dress.

It isn't always easy to shepherd people, but Morning Coat never failed; and these two stood in the throng of the lounge together for a moment saying a few words more before parting, when a short man in White

Waistcoat and Butterfly Tie, very glorious, showed in the offing. He was walking towards them but looking away to the right, when he bumped into them ; apologies, brief introduction—a moment of small talk in which White Waistcoat said something to Morning Coat.

"You heard about the Bourrot ?" Then he stopped short as having said a word too much, glanced at the Duke and hesitated.

"It's all right," laughed Morning Coat. "He's just heard. I've told him."

"Oh !" said White Waistcoat, much relieved. "Well, I'm afraid it'll be all over London by to-morrow night—but meanwhile . . ." he looked round furtively ; then murmured hurriedly, "someone's told Vurry Norbolt, and she's on to it !"

He smiled mysteriously and was off.

The Duke thought it was time to dress, and so did Morning Coat : he went off merrily : and if you will believe me, as he passed White Waistcoat in the throng he winked. But the Duke moved off by himself more slowly.

He put on no turn of speed till he was safe inside his own door. Then, with the rapidity of a large terrier, he leapt upon his Emergency Box, unlocked it, took out what he humorously called the Iron Ration—it was a stout buff envelope full of notes—took the back stairs two at a time (disdaining lifts and their publicity), popped out by the side door into mews where no one watched, ran to a taxi in forty-two seconds, gave the address of Gabriel in Chelsea and promised double fare.

As he raced along the Embankment (cursing the blocks at the Bridges) his excited brain had formed no scheme. Money could do anything. Money always had . . . Oh! If only Mr. Gabriel were still about at such an hour!

In twelve minutes he was in Chelsea. He stopped the taxi two hundred yards from where they had told him Gabriel held his shop. He dismissed the cab, saw it safely disappear, and then ran down the side street to the bow-window they had described. The shop was shut up, but its owner might be in, and the one thing needful was to be first in the field. He hammered at the door.

He hammered again. There was no answer. The third time he hammered continuously, regardless of consequences. He was determined. A window crept up in an attic; an aged crone first told him what she thought of him, and then, to his inquiries, that Mr. Gabriel wouldn't be there till the morning. What hour? Never before eight! What was his private address? Down crashed the attic window with emphasis.

There was nothing for it: he must wait. But he went back to his hotel in a fever. Suppose Gabriel had taken it off with him? Suppose he'd gone straight to Vurry's? Suppose Vurry had it now, at that hour, in her house, safe and sound?

He got very little sleep that night, with Iron Rations

under his pillow and confused visions of misfortune haunting his mind whenever he dosed. But the interval was of advantage to him. For, waking very early in the summer morning, he had time to make a plan.

He was up and dressed by six, and in the stillness, at his sitting-room table, pencil in hand and the gorgeously embossed sheets of Plantagenet note-paper before him, he reviewed the case.

In the first place, Gabriel might have got rid of the Bourrot already—probably to Verecundia "Oh! Agony!" He put this horrid thought away.

In the second place, suppose Gabriel still had it, the picture wasn't Gabriel's to dispose of. It was Bensington's. If Gabriel sold it he sold it as stolen goods—for a man in the trade couldn't pretend not to have heard of the masterpiece—and that meant Dartmoor. It would need something enormous to make an elderly man risk, say, three years odd at the least and, say, eight at the most. He might not do it at any price. The Duke sucked his pencil and frowned; it had never yet occurred to him that there were limits to the power of money. He leant back in his chair and looked at the ceiling for advice.

The ceiling gave him a reminder which brought him back to hard thinking again.

Even if Gabriel fell (as his namesake's colleague, Lucifer, had fallen), even if Gabriel "succumbed to pressure," ran the risk and handed over the Masterpiece for cash down, what was Hardham to do with it? He couldn't own it publicly. It was stolen goods again. Well, anyhow, that kept it out of Vurry's hands . . .

But, wait a bit! . . . Even so he'd have the weight of it on his mind for life. . . . He might destroy it? . . . But he'd read too many detective stories (he read nothing else except the Stock Exchange, Police Court news, and racing colmns for his gambling). Murder will out. You drown the corpse and it floats, or you burn it and there's a bit of charred bone, or you bury it and the earth gives up its dead. Anyway, his life afterwards would be poisoned with anxiety. . . . It was a hell of a puzzle!

His Grace was now chewing the pencil vigorously, and not a word of plan had he jotted down. He would wait for developments. . . . No! by Gawd he couldn't—and he thumped the table. Naw! Developments? That meant Vurry's snatching up the durn thing under his nose. He glared at the bronze statuette on the mantelpiece as though it were the robust Marchioness herself, and he snarled at it. "Vurry shan't have it! Curfew shall not ring to-night! No, Sur!"

That was why he'd come over to London. That was why he was here. He weren't whipped yet. . . . And once more he sought counsel from above, from the ceiling, and once more the ceiling was gracious and deigned to reveal.

The Inspiration was so sudden that Hardham was

almost awed. In a moment he was vaguely jotting down his schemes. Of course! It was obvious! He must *borrow* the Bourrot. Not buy it: *borrow* it: borrow it just to look at—for a short fixed term—with a full receipt and written promise of return—with a written promise also to inform Bensington that he had borrowed it. There! That was it! No risk of prison for old Gabriel—only an unpleasant scene with Bensington and perhaps the loss of a business connection . . . Oh! yes! It would want some doing; a big enough sum down to tempt the old dealer to anything so irregular. Yes, irregular—but after all not criminal. At any rate, it was a feasible plan with every chance of success.

Once he had that canvas he was in command. Possession was everything. Even if Bensington wouldn't sell (and Hardham guessed he would! Money talks!), there would be delays . . . . . and (here he chuckled) it might be stolen *again* . . . there were all sorts of ways.

He grasped the chewed pencil with decision and rapidly jotted down half a dozen headings in his pocket-book. Then he pulled towards him two sheets of the Plantagenet paper (with its three golden leopards of Anjou on a field Azure, quartering the fleur de lys argent) and wrote in ink the two decisive documents.

One was a receipt for the "*Ame Bourgeoise*," canvas by the late M. Bourrot, lent to him, Duke of Emonsillado, etc., for the space of three days only, that is to say, up to noon of Thursday, June the 27th, and thereafter returnable upon demand to Mr. Gabriel, 84 Cheyne Row, Chelsea.

The other was a brief clear note to Sir Henry Bensington, congratulating him on the recovery of the Masterpiece, informing him of his own action, saying that he held the picture only for purpose of inspection and would, of course, return it at once if the owner desired it, admitting that he had taken a liberty in borrowing it, and offering to purchase it at once for £20,000, as Sir Henry had suggested. It was misspelt and awkwardly phrased, but to the point. He signed the documents, put them separately into two envelopes, addressed one to Gabriel, one to Bensington, blotted them, and carefully stowed them into his breast-pocket.

The Duke looked at his watch, it was close on seven. He had spent a full hour in reaching that decision. But the sigh he gave was a sigh of deep content. He began to think himself a genius. Oh! They were cunning and the trick had been hard to play; but he was a match for them all! With his exultation was mixed some superstitious awe for the source of his inspiration. If it were not the ceiling, it was at least from Above.

Then he would wait no longer, early as was the hour. He strolled out through the deserted streets, picked up a crawling cab within half a mile and got him to Chelsea. There he paced slowly up and down before the closely-shuttered bow-windows, awaiting his prey, congratulating himself on the recovery of the Masterpiece.

From the end of the street a policeman watched that figure with suspicion. Hardham bore in his gait the (to the Force) unmistakable brand, the imprint of Those-who-have-been-in-trouble, Those-who-have-been-put-through-it. On the other hand, it was corrected by many years of wealth and the subject was dressed by a very good tailor. His soft hat was particularly expensive. The officer decided to watch, but do no more.

It was a long wait, but Hardham had determined to run no risk of being forestalled. Not till just after eight did Mr. Gabriel appear. He bowed to the Duke as he put his key into the lock. "Good morning, your Grace," he said.

"Aw. Ye knaw me, do yer?" said the grandee, half taken aback, half flattered. But no matter. He was giving his name in a moment anyhow.

"Oh yes, your Grace!" with a respectful smile. "I'm afraid people of your Grace's eminence must expect to be recognized. Pray come in. What can I do for you?"

"Yer vurry kind," answered the Nobleman as he got into the little shop and sank down on a Queen Anne settee. "Won't yer be seated, Mr. Gabriel?"

"Thank you, your Grace . . ." He took a Chippendale, pulled it up and added again. "What can I do for you?"

"Wal, Ah'm not one of your mist'ry men, Mr. Gabriel. Ah'll talk plain. Ye've got that Bourrot . . .

Mayn't pronounce it right, but ye know what ah mean. What they call d'Masterpiece."

"You are quite right, your Grace," answered old Mr. Gabriel quietly. "It's back there in the Inner room in my safe. I don't wonder you're having heard of its recovery, though it's early yet. I've only had custody of it since yesterday early afternoon." (He had a strict regard for truth in such details.) "A man whom I'd never seen brought it here under his arm, and wanted five pounds for it. Unfortunately, as I unpacked it, a client came in and no doubt that's how the news got about. But no matter. I gave the man his five pounds in odd change, and asked no questions. He went out again at once with the money, and I've not seen him since, and not likely to." (The Duke here nodded with a wise and approving smile.) "We're used to this kind of thing in the trade, your Grace. I've no doubt the man was under dismissal by the Receiver (Dodgers we call them), and thought he'd have a revenge and a little packet for himself as well. We make it a point not to ask. It's a necessary policy. He had no idea of the value. Don't think I was compounding a felony."

"Naw! Naw!" cried the Duke encouragingly, "cern'ly not! . . . Now, Mr. Gabriel," and here he fixed the old man with a glare, "Ah've come here to make ye a Proposition."

Mr. Gabriel rose to his feet.

"Your Grace," he said, "we must understand each other. I am in close business relations with Sir Henry

Bensington. He is a friend of many years' standing, if I may use the term of one so much my superior. Even if that were not so the '*Ame Bourgeoise*' . . ."

"That's t'name!" cried Hardham. "Ah'm not much at these foreign words, so Ah didn't say it! G'wan."

". . . The '*Ame Bourgeoise*' is Sir Henry Bensington's property. I have not even agency in the matter. I tried to communicate with him the moment I saw what it was, but he was out of town. When he returns, in a day or two, I shall let him know at once."

"Ye don't take me, Mr. Gabriel," answered the Duke earnestly. "Ah'm not here to suggest anny such thing. Gawd forbid!"

Mr. Gabriel sat down in great relief.

"Naw! When Ah say Ah've a Proposition to put to ye, it's the wrawng word p'raps. . . . All Ah want ye to do fer me's this. I want yer to let me look at the picture jest fur two days—or mebbe three. . . ." He put up his hand to check an interruption. "Now listen t'*me*. Ah've a reason. Ah'm a purchaser. Sir Harry'll tell you that. Ah've made him a firm offer, and so he'll tell ye himself when ye see him. And Ah said to him while it wurr still on show: 'Ye let me have it a day or two, so my friends can see it private, and Ah'll pay beforehand; *now*, if you like; only then it was still at Martin's. Oh, he'll tell ye! We're old friends, and he'll get no better price, and he knows it. Ef he were here in this room, he'd say, 'Cern'ly!' That's what he'd say!"

There was a long pause, at the end of which old Mr. Gabriel spoke with lowered eyes.

"Of course, your Grace, we all trust you. There's no question of anything else. There's no harm in the suggestion. None at all. Only it's not *customary*. I believe you implicitly. Every word you say. But *if* there *was* any misadventure, if you hadn't quite understood him, or if Sir Henry preferred it to remain with him for the moment, before the transfer." He hesitated, then he went on. "Frankly, it puts me in a difficult position. I can't afford to offend Sir Henry even in a small detail like this . . . I'm not a rich man, and his connection is worth half my takings to me . . . at least half. And he's very imperious, as you know."

The Grandee saw that Mr. Gabriel was yielding.

"Ah've considered all that," he said generously, "an' Ah've brought with me" (he pulled out the Buff envelope) "what ye may take as Ernest money if ye like, or keep what part ye think fit for ye trouble and risk. It's only fair. Jest ten per cent. of what Ah understand he agreed for. Ah can't say fairer! . . . Count it," he concluded.

"Oh! There's no need." Mr. Gabriel seemed confused.

"Aw! Count it, man!"

And Mr. Gabriel counted it. He made his hand shake cleverly before he had finished. Five notes for a hundred pounds each, ten for fifty, twenty-five twenties and fifty tens . . . two thousand pounds. He put them back into the envelope.

"Naw," pushing it back. "An' Ah won't take a receipt. Ah trust ye as ye trust me—an' as Harry does. As Ah say. Yew take jest what ye think fit fer yer trouble, and ef there *is* any mistake and he's short about it, why it'll compensate ye, and that's only right. But if there ain't (an' there won't be), ye can give him jest what ye like of it as Ernest to count off. He's only got to let me know how much . . . Bless ye! Ah can *afford* it!"

"Yes, your Grace . . . certainly . . . certainly . . . of course you can." Mr. Gabriel held the envelope as though still hesitating. "But it would be more regular . . ."

The Duke smiled again wisely. "Ah've considered that too!" He pulled out the two documents. "These'll make it all fixed up tight an' as right es rain!" he said.

Mr. Gabriel read them both carefully one after the other and his face lifted.

"Yes," he said in a much more confident tone, "that makes all the difference! Of course, it's only a formality. But a written acknowledgment of *loan*, and a fixed term—just three days only, and to be called for at any moment—that makes all the difference! Yes, and your own letter to Sir Henry . . . shall I give it him when I see him? Perhaps you'll have done with the picture by the time he's back?"

"Yep; give it him and show him the receipt. Now we're square?"

"Yes, your Grace. Yes. Certainly . . . really, I'm afraid I must have seemed a little punctilious."

"There! There!" assured the millionaire good-naturedly, "an' now Ah'll jest take it as it is, if ye'll wrap it up for me."

Mr. Gabriel went away to his safe, came back with the Masterpiece, and carefully packed it before the Duke's eager eyes. Then a cab was telephoned for, they bade courteous farewells, and the "*Ame Bourgeoise*" rolled safely off, and its triumphant possessor, having locked it safely away, ate ravenously, in the Plantagenet, a breakfast wickedly delayed.

CHAPTER XV

EVEN while the genial Grandee of Spain was devouring his breakfast at the Plantagenet with the gestures and grimaces of the Greater Carnivora, the aged and courteous but determined Mr. Gabriel was closeted with the distinguished Head of his profession. Sir Henry was extremely pleased. He did not often betray emotion, but on this occasion he went so far as to take Mr. Gabriel's hand and shake it warmly.

"Very well done, Gabriel!" he said. "Very well done indeed!" Then again: "Very well done! I couldn't have done it better myself!"—and that from Henry Bensington was very high praise. For, like Nelson, Gnatho, Nero, and a few other characters, he knew his own value.

"I 'll tell you what you have done for me, for I think you ought to know. Fifteen hundred will exactly recoup my expenses—and that was all I wanted. The balance you shall have for yourself. You deserve it. I would not have taken more, I don't think it's fair to sell more than one of the two at the full price—do you?" he asked frankly, as one honest man of another.

Mr. Gabriel coughed slightly.

"Well," he said, "of course, every man must be his

own judge in things of this kind. I am sure it is very generous of you, Sir Henry—very generous indeed."

"Now then, Gabriel," said Sir Henry, beaming with the exceptional good humour of the moment, "draw up your chair and I'll sit down here, and we'll make a plan of campaign—eh ?"

"As you will, Sir Henry ; as you will."

The chairs were drawn up, and the master mind tackled its problem, as a good wrestler grips his opponent to make sure of the throw. I have seen certain commanders in the Great War considering all the elements of a complicated affair without the use of a map, so vividly could they use the map they had within—so it was with Henry Bensington : without jotting down a single note, he had marshalled the whole position.

"My first intention, Gabriel, is to sell the remaining one to the lady. That is clear—you probably guessed that ?"

Mr. Gabriel nodded.

"Well, *then*," continued Sir Henry Bensington, "there will inevitably arise a conflict. There is no way out of it. The only reason that fearful fellow Hardy wanted the thing at all was to put poor Lady Norbolt's nose out of joint. When he hears she's got it (and I shall take good care that everybody knows) he will protest. He will write to me, he will certainly make a row with Lady Norbolt. Shall I tell you what I think will follow ?"

"What ?" said Mr. Gabriel deferentially, though he knew quite as well as Bensington.

"A lawsuit!" said the Master of the Picture Market, crashing his hand down upon the table. "Now, then; there are risks in everything, and Nothing venture, Nothing have. There are two tales to be told. I want you to keep the thing clear in your head, for we must have nothing going wrong. First, we must settle what these two pictures are, and how each of us came by them. That's in the ordinary way of business."

Mr. Gabriel nodded.

"But later on"—he looked steadily at his companion, and spoke in graver and lower tones—"there will have to be evidence given on oath in Court, if it comes to Court; and as I said, I think it will."

Mr. Gabriel nodded again.

"Very well." Bensington went on with decision, the fingers of both hands strongly interclasped on the table before him. "First, as to how we got these pictures. You have told me how it stands between you and this Duke fellow. A man came in hurriedly, wanted five pounds for it, went out, and you have no way of tracing him?"

"That's right," said Mr. Gabriel.

"Well, now, I'll tell you how I came by *my* copy. I was looking casually at a bunch of parcels in the front office when I saw one rather small, the shape of which seemed familiar. I opened it, and it was the Masterpiece. No one seems to have any idea of how it got there. Perhaps somebody left it, perhaps I had forgotten to put it into the safe after all, and only thought I had done so by a sort of automatic gesture. At any rate, there it is."

Mr. Gabriel interrupted gently.

"But my copy, which the Duke has borrowed, Sir Henry, is the original work. It was stolen from your safe. I will stake my professional reputation on it. It is unmistakable."

Henry Bensington in his delight at his colleague's intelligence nearly crowed. Only dignity forbade him that expression of joy.

"By Gad, Gabriel!" he cried, "I do believe yours is the only mind on a level with mine! You have said exactly what was on the tip of my tongue. That's it! That's it precisely! When you had got it you saw at once from your own wide knowledge of such things, your expert acquaintance with the whole school, and particularly with Bourrot's body of work, that what had been so mysteriously left at your door was the original."

Gabriel nodded.

"Right!" went on Sir Henry. "Now, Gabriel, *I* am equally convinced from *my* expert knowledge, etc., etc., etc."—he was so pleased with himself that he almost laughed—"I will stake my professional reputation also upon the authenticity of the copy *I* have. Yours is a miserable fake, and the Duke is welcome to it as far as I am concerned. Is that clear?"

"Yes, Sir Henry, yes, certainly—quite clear."

There was just that little interval of time without

speech which separates the common and daily from the sacred and perilous. Then Henry Bensington went on in that other, graver tone:

"If or when it comes to the witness box, Gabriel—these stories must stand."

"Exactly, Sir Henry," said Mr. Gabriel firmly.

"No cross-examination will shake them. It's your reputation against mine. And it will be for the judge and jury to decide. You will be respectful to me, of course, and I to you—we each owe it to the other; but we differ as black and white in the matter of the authenticity of the two copies. There! That's settled."

Mr. Gabriel saw that the interview was at an end, asked whether he should repeat the plan to show that he had it clearly, since of course nothing could be written. Bensington heard him accurately restate every point, and then before dismissing him thanked him again for his admirable discharge of duty.

"As I told you, you have just recouped me. There was £500 each to my distinguished colleagues, French and Italian, there was a very well-earned payment I have made to my agents, and there have been sundry other little out-of-pocket expenses, as you know. I'll call the whole thing fifteen hundred, as I said, and there's five hundred for you, Gabriel, five hundred for you, five hundred for you!"

Mr. Gabriel bowed, very deeply, as though to Royalty. It was a great deal more than he had expected, and he began to murmur thanks.

"Not at all, not at all, my dear Gabriel," said Bensington, showing him to the door. "You deserve it."

As he went back alone to his desk, he tackled by himself what was much the worst point in the whole affair, the heart of the peril. Four human beings would be privy to the fact that he, Bensington, and Gabriel his colleague, had lied in any common statement or letter they might make or write on these matters, and if such statement appeared as evidence in Court, these four human beings would each know that Bensington had committed perjury. Now perjury is punishable by law. These four human beings were M. Caen, Signor Alessandria, the Bright Young Artist and the Temporary Odd Man.

For a moment Henry Bensington hesitated as to whether the servant at the inn or her sister, of whom he had been told the story, made a fifth and a sixth; but he decided that they could be eliminated. No one would know of them or wish to sub-pœna them, and people in that class never incriminate themselves: their one desire would be to keep out of the hands of the police.

But what of the Four?

He covered his eyes with his hand and let his judgment form. Yes, he was sure of *his* two, Appleton and Ranford. Each was still young, each was well paid, each had been amply rewarded in other matters, their part in which they would not care to have divulged; each was thoroughly dependent upon him by interest and by fear.

Now for Caen and Alessandria. Bensington knew these worthies by heart, and in detail, from the cradle to the present day. He had them card-indexed like all the others and a whole dossier of their movements and little adventures: all they had done throughout their interesting lives.

No! He could be quite sure of them. They could only betray him by betraying themselves, and once they should allow it to be suspected, let alone obvious, that they had taken part in a theft, not even the short memory of the public nor the natural kindness of the Administration for men of their sort could save them from ruin. Their rich clients would trust them no more. He rapidly resurveyed the field, sprang to his feet with his judgment confirmed—he was safe.

While he was still in this mood of confidence, only a few minutes after he had come to his fixed decision that there was no necessity for further reproach, payment or even threat in the case of any of the Four, he was handed a note which had come by hand.

Once again it was an envelope bearing the gorgeously embossed crest of the Plantagenet, and the uncultured hand of the Duque de Emonsillado. It was marked: "Bearer Waits!" He read the contents with a pursed smile on his firm mouth:

"Dear old Harry,

"I must make a cleen brest of it. Wen I heard your pichure was found I went and borrowed it you know where and who from now I've gotten it here quite safe but see here Harry you take my orfer, left it in riting with you know who" (*the terms of that writing positively winked at Bensington as he read this*) "it's firm an good an you can have it at cawl today if you like by return. I fixed for the big check passing through and made the bank wise an they may expect it any minnit an here it is."

And sure enough, on looking back into the crested envelope, Henry Bensington saw that cheque, an open one: and the sum upon it was £20,000. He opened the door and called out: "Ask who ever brought that note to wait just a moment," and scribbled off at top speed these simple words:

"MY DEAR HARDY,

"Don't make a fool of yourself. And don't take me for a robber. Here is your cheque back again. The picture you've got isn't Bourrot's. It's not the Masterpiece at all. I have heard all about it. It's a copy, and in my judgment, a worthless one.

"Yours,

"HARRY."

He fastened down the envelope, addressed it to His Grace the Duke of Emonsillado; and he sent it off by the same messenger who had brought the first letter. Within a quarter of an hour he had sent off by a messenger of his own a note to Lady Norbolt—short, simple and to the point:

"MY DEAR LADY NORBOLT,

"You will be glad to hear that the picture which was lost has been recovered. You will have seen that the value at which I estimated it in the advertisements for its recovery, and in the articles which have appeared in the Press, was that of your own offer, £20,000.

"If you will ring me up and let me know when you will be round here, the transaction can be completed at once to your satisfaction and to mine.

"Yours,

"HENRY BENSINGTON.

"P.S.—It would be wiser on all accounts and for both our interests that you should bring a witness."

When this projectile, after describing a graceful parabola, exploded in the heart of Verecundia Norbolt, it first shook her with delight, then with hesitation. But two emotions combined and settled her into decision. She summoned Ardee imperiously, told her the news in half a dozen words, and added:

"Ah've made up me mind. Put on ye' things, telephone to him, tell them to send round the car . . . the Baker'll be best, it goes slicker through traffic—and then come 'long. Oh, yes, and bring me me cheque-book, and just drop this round at the Bank."

She bent down, too hurried to sit, and dashed off a note telling that Institution to expect what was coming to them. On their way—and it was a very short journey—the Great Lady informed Ardee of her resolution in tones which admitted of no argument ; and you may be sure that Ardee enthusiastically agreed.

"You won't feel a sum like that, darling," she said, cuddling up to her protectress. "Think what a glory it will be to have it safe and sound ! You must show it, now and then."

"That's all right, dearest," answered the Head of the Family, as she would have called herself. "Ah've got a plan for that—Ah'll tell ye."

And they were at Henry Bensington's door.

The interview was short—shorter than Bensington himself had anticipated. She wrote out the cheque then and there, and received the Picture with due solemnity. She graciously extended her hand. Sir Henry accepted it with an almost equal if less obvious grace. He was a difficult man to patronize.

And so the thing ended, and you may think that with Verecundia in possession, my story also is coming to an end—if you do, you are wrong.

CHAPTER XVI

WHEN the Duque de Emonsillado received Sir Henry Bensington's curt but familiar and sufficient note, even before he had read it, from the moment he cut the envelope and caught sight of the pink of the returned cheque within, his perturbation was extreme. When he had read it his perturbation increased. And he asked himself, as he was entitled to do after his experience of mankind in various climates and different forms of practice, what the great idea might be.

It would be flattery to pretend that the Duke had any knowledge of pictures in any school whatsoever, let alone of modern symbolism. He took out the canvas from its locked security, put it in a strong light before the window, gazed at it intently with his head cocked to one side; and it told him nothing. And curse it all! Even if Bensington did not believe the thing to be genuine, what possible motive could he have for refusing twenty thousand pounds? . . . Perhaps someone had offered more? If one may throw a sprat to catch a whale, one may throw a whale to catch the great sea serpent. . . . No, that wouldn't wash. If someone else was biting, he wouldn't have repudiated the picture —just the other way. . . .

The Duke frowned a puzzled frown. He could make nothing of it. Anyhow, there was *one* thing he could do. He could clinch his own position right down good and hard. He spent between half and three quarters of an hour in getting hold of Borstal, whose voice he heard at last on the other end of the wire—in not too good a temper ; but Hardy soothed him. For as between millionaires of the same type, Borstal could not but be moved by the familiar " one of us " feeling. Yes, Borstal would see to it. It should go into the social column. The Duke thanked him sincerely, and offered to give a little extra tip to the poor devil who wrote the paragraphs. But Borstal would have none of that. " It spoils them," he said. And so it does. What on earth would happen to Borstal if the snake Self-respect should raise its poisonous head among his staff ?

Therefore it was that on the very next day, the moment the pubs. opened in Fleet Street, the more Bohemian half of Lothario entered The Green Monkey and the saloon bar thereof, quaffed the first honest beer of the day from a huge tankard, and smudged his Par. down on a particularly dirty block.

" I met the Duque de Emonsillado the other day ; he told me he had run over to London to see his numerous English friends, and to take advantage of the Season, as he does every year—for he is at heart an Englishman, in spite of his high rank in a friendly foreign country.

Alcoholic influence exerted upon one half of Lothario, resulting in literary creation by same

"He told me, by the way, that he had just purchased Bourrot's famous Masterpiece, the '*Ame Bourgeoise*' which we have all been hearing about since its recent loss. How it was recovered he was not free to tell me. But it is good news for every lover of Art. And I think I may respectfully add, for every friend of His Grace—and they are legion."

He read it over. It read fine. He had another pint on the strength of it. The barmaid asked him with haughty kindness what lie he was telling now, and he answered, "Never you mind, duckie, it's not about you!" Nor did that goddess resent the address, such a favourite with the ladies was the genial fellow in the world which he adorned.

* * * * *

Meanwhile, in far Golders Green, in that very respectable villa, and sipping the first of his third cup of coffee that morning, the other half of Lothario was searching his poor little brain for something to write. A suggestion came (as it often did) with the entry of his formidable spouse.

"Not finished yet?" she snapped, "and I've left you half an hour!"

"Oh, my dear—not twenty minutes!" murmured the poor little fellow.

"Well, upon my word! Archibald, it's a wonder I bear with you! I'm sure if I've been away a minute I've been away the better part of an hour—doing work *you* ought to be doing. Trying to get that wretched girl to . . . I declare, you've got not a word down on that paper!"

"Well, my dear, I've been thinking. . . ."

"Thinking?" shot out the hard, thin voice with dreadful menace. "*Thinking?* Really, Archibald, I don't know *how* I manage to bear with you at all! . . ."

"Well, my dear, I can't think of anything to think of."

But he was interrupted.

"Well, for one thing, the Marchioness of Norbolt" (the lady pronounced it in a fine rotund fashion, as though she had some property in it) "she's bought that picture—they've found it. She got it yesterday. You knew that, I suppose?"

"Oh, my dear," answered the unoffending spouse, "we can't be sure of that, you know. We only heard it from the curate, and he himself said he wasn't sure, as he had only heard it from Mrs. Gatwick, and he himself said he didn't know how she got hold of news like that, because . . . well, you know, it's not her world."

"Don't talk rubbish, Archibald," snapped his commander-in-chief. "Write that paragraph down at once. It'll be almost too late as it is—do you know what the time is?"

"Oh, dear, yes," said poor Archibald. "There! All right—I'll do it."

"I'll be back in ten minutes," tapped out the inexorable

tongue. "And I'll take it down myself, to make certain that you don't lose it with some of your drunken companions!"

"Oh, my dear," said the shocked and maligned master of the house, "my dear!"

"Don't you 'my dear' me!" said the lady. "You get to your work!"

Archibald got to his work. He sighed pitifully—he was a scrupulous little man, besides which, getting wrong things in a Par. was dangerous. However, there was one course much more dangerous, and that was to disobey—so down it went:

> "I dined with the Marchioness of Norbolt yesterday (what a hostess she is!), and she told me a bit of news which will bring gladness not only to her innumerable friends, but to every lover of Art at home and abroad. Bourrot's Masterpiece has been found, and as might have been expected, this greatest of Art judges and Art lovers has become the possessor of it. I am afraid I committed an indiscretion when I asked her the conditions under which she had obtained it, but she tapped me archly with her lorgnette" (*was it Lorgnette or Lorgnon?—he wasted three minutes in an agony of doubt: looked it up first in the Etiquette Book and then in Boulter's Dictionary of Universal Information, and couldn't find it in either. He was still hesitating when a too-well-known step as of marching Fate was heard upon the stair, and he hurriedly concluded:*) "She told

Marital influence exercised upon the other half of Lothario, resulting in literary creation by same

me I must not ask questions, but I was very proud when she added that I might go and see the Masterpiece at an early date. And I shall certainly avail myself of that invitation. I hope you envy me."

"Have you finished it, Archibald?" came the Voice from the door.

"Yes, my dear," his own voice humbly replied.

"Well, give it me. Can't you see I can't open the door? I've got my hands full. . . . Thanks to having to do all the housework!"

He dutifully went and deposited the bit of copy in an envelope upon the tray which the lady was holding, filled with crockery for the luncheon-table.

"It's killing me having to do three women's work every day," she said. "If you were a man you wouldn't stand by and see your wife slave herself to death while you idled away your time with that dirty Fleet Street crowd!"

"Oh, my dear!" he protested again. But she could bear no more of it. Her cup was full—which was also true of his, by the way, for he had had no time to finish his coffee. He allowed time for the apparelling of that majestic though somewhat angular form, heard the door slam with a profound sensation of relief, and was confident of this at least in a difficult and perilous world, that Olivia (for such was the name of his life's companion and stay) would not be the woman to lose a thing or to fail to deliver it. He only hoped the news in it was all right!

* * * * *

All these paragraphs went in! Golders Green and Bohemia, both halves of "Lothario" hobnobbing with the great. They contradicted themselves and didn't make sense. They gave the same picture to two separate people. But the sub-editor, who was sleepy drunk and short of copy, passed them. He got the sack; and the 2½ million readers of *The Howl* learnt that not only had the Duke of Emonsillado bought the Masterpiece, but Lady Norbolt as well!

* * * * *

The next morning the Duke's friend Mr. Capstan, that well-known figure at Tattersall's, was sitting at the Duke's breakfast-table in the Plantagenet prior to a walk around among the gee-gees. His host was reading with a smile the first two Paragraphs about himself and the Bourrot, when Capstan looked up, startled by a sudden exclamation. Hardham, Duque de Emonsillado in the Barony of Castile, and of Manuada and Bo in that of Aragon, had *The Howl* clenched in his left hand and was viciously slapping it down before him. His right fist menaced the air, his face was working with passion, and from a mouth opened very wide indeed were pouring the strangest howls of rage.

"Aw! Ter Hell with her! May she burn! Aw, that's it, is it? Aw, my Gawd, when Ah get her! Thet man Borstal's crazy!" And with that the grasping fingers actually tore through the strong fine paper of Lord Borstal's organ of public opinion. Then, dealing with it as though it were the unfortunate Verecundia,

Renewed and Excessive Protest by a Spanish Grandee against the criticisms of an Anglo-Saxon Peeress

he savagely tore it in two, still roaring his anathemas of rage.

"Ah'll prorsecoot!" he shouted. "Ah'll heve her jailed! Ah'll . . ." He ground his teeth with savage snarls; and then, at the end of the orgasm, choked.

Capstan deferentially patted him on the back. That only made him worse. He recovered his breath and began a universal commination service, extending to Capstan himself, and all the peoples of these islands, to goddurned French painting fools and bloody Mayfair robbers, and all those gutterhags who thought themselves so grand; he raved on in reminiscences of various indignities connected with their common youth, his and Vurry's by the far Pacific Seas, and then took to blaspheming at large till he was quite exhausted.

"Ah'll prorsecoot!" he repeated. "Ah'll prorsecoot! The word seemed to relieve him somewhat, as though he was actively engaged in the squeezing to destruction the abominated Vurry. "Ah'll teach her! Ah'll larn her!" And then, by way of finale, he stamped his foot on that mighty voice of England for which Lord Borstal was responsible, stopped, snatched it up, crumpled it with his strong hands into a ball as hard as wood, and hurled it through the open window: whence it fell too violently upon the astounded head of a godly Lady Missionary who was descending the narrow side street upon an errand of mercy, to nobble a poor and wicked man of whom the police had need.

* * * * *

At last, but not till fully twenty minutes had passed, the great amateur of modern art, had so far recovered himself (and exhaustion took no small part in that recovery) that he was able to answer consecutively the questions Mr. Capstan thought it only decent to put, in a voice full of sympathy and old friendship.

Yes, Capstan had guessed right. It was the picture. It was thet bitch, thet . . . but I will not sully your ears, radiant reader, with the further epithet he applied to so distinguished a member of your sex. She had had the gall to get in front, had she? Wall, she'd soon find she wouldn't stay there! She'd gotten the Bourrot?—Naw! *He'd* gotten it! All she'd gotten was a bloody fake! He'd show her up, he would! Naw, he was in no mood for durned horses, blast 'em! He was going to his lawyer, he was. Pretty darn quick, too. And Capstan might come with him.

Very pleased was Capstan to note that this essential friend was so far mollified. Eagerly did he accept. Clapping on their hats, and seizing their walking-sticks, the one with a deferential gesture, the other with a military grasp, as though to slay with it the arch-villainess of the Peerage, they strode forth on their way to Lincoln's Inn.

CHAPTER XVII

It began with a general announcement in the Press that Verecundia, Marchioness of Norbolt, had purchased Bourrot's famous Masterpiece the "*Ame Bourgeoise*," which had happily been recovered. It went on with a Lawyer's letter in the Press protesting that the "*Ame Bourgeoise*" was the property of His Grace the Duke of Emonsillado, and demanding a retractation. It continued with a counter-affirmation in the Press by the Lawyers of the Marchioness of Norbolt.

It ended with a claim for damages and a counter-claim, and the case of Emonsillado v. Norbolt, defendant counter - claiming, was set down for hearing after prodigious delay.

The Solicitors by appointment to His Grace the Duke of Emonsillado were fortunate enough to retain for their Counsel at a mountainous fee no less an advocate than Sir Anselm Atterleigh, K.C., whose gigantic income was fully half that with which he was commonly credited. It was perhaps this ample revenue which had prevented his taking a seat on the Bench. He was a man of good birth, grace and refinement, a collector of china and a deeply religious man, especially attached to liturgical music.

The firm which had, for now more than eighty years, protected (and robbed) the estates and interests of the Walburton family and the Peerage of Norbolt were so dexterous as to retain for Counsel, at a fee of startling dimensions, Sir Rory Hawlboy himself, a King's Counsel whose immense earnings were even larger than was generally believed. It was probably a distaste to lowering his annual receipts by three-quarters which had caused him to refuse a Judgeship. He was a man of no birth, grace or refinement, in no way moved by religion, but the possessor of a voice like an angry bull, and a fine indifference to the quality of liquor so long as he was secure of quantity in it.

It is an example of that noble detachment for which the Bar is famous that Sir Anselm, the Duke's Counsel, would have shuddered to approach the strange world of his client and was a regular guest at Norbolt House, while Sir Rory was a familiar associate of the Duke's world of touts, drunkards, boxers, gamblers and sharpers, whether in England or on the Riviera. Yet it was certain that Verecundia's interests were as safe in the powerful fist of Sir Rory as Hardham's in the delicate but firm fingers of Sir Anselm. Indeed, it seemed impossible that, with such genius at work on either side, both should not triumph.

With these great men were associated as juniors Mr. Pott and Mr. Smith (Yes ? Why not ? I hope there is nothing odd or disgraceful in the name Smith ?), who played but little part in the Case beyond pocketing the modest fees marked on their briefs. Indeed, were it not for the touching and beautiful custom whereby wealthy clients are expected to support juniors, they need never have appeared at all. Yet it was well they did, as it all worked in as practice for the profession they adorned and to which each brought his own peculiar gifts, destined in later years to yield renown and wealth; Mr. Pott a happy self-confidence, Mr. Smith an appearance of pure guilessness invaluable to all whose calling may demand, on occasion, a certain hypocrisy.

The Judge before whom the case *Emonsillado v. Norbolt* (Norbolt counter-claiming) was to be heard was no less a personage than Mr. Justice Dove, with whose equal mind and serene urbane demeanour the public were familiar; for it was ten years since his elevation to the Bench after letting down poor Bill Atkins over the Home Secretary's criminal libel case. It was a wise choice, for Mr. Dove was not making much at the Bar, and even a Judge's income was a fortune to him. Moreover, he was passionless, and therefore rigidly impartial in all cases free from social or political complications. No one was better fitted to preside over a conflict of interest between equals.

The special jury empanelled for the occasion were as happily fitted for their task of deciding the authenticity of a Symbolist French Picture. Mr. Balchin, the foreman, was a Grocer, in a good way of business. Miss Wiseman, a spinster, had read many modern works of

Mr. Pott, Junior to Sir Anselm. (He played no great part in the famous case)

Mr. Smith, Junior to Sir Rory Hawlboy. (He played no great part in the famous case)

fiction and had even herself painted in water-colour. Mr. Richards was an accountant. Among the others were a horse healer, a market gardener, a gentleman who let out pleasure boats upon the Thames, a substantial publican and a Mrs. Large (a widow).

Sir Anselm (with whom Mr. Pott) rose to open the case for the Duke in a crowded court. The public interest excited by the original exhibition of the "*Ame Bourgeoise*," its disappearance, its reputed double recovery and the violent dispute upon the two rival examples, had survived the Long Vacation; and Lord Borstal and Sir Charles Holloway had seen to it that the fever should be fed. A long queue had stood in the November rain for hours, awaiting the opening of the public galleries. The well was packed with the more privileged, and "Peach" Daggetty had been accommodated with that seat on the Bench which is customary to Ladies of position and curiosity. Unfortunately, she got bored and left early, before the second act.

Sir Anselm began in that low, reserved tone which is so effective with a Jury. He knew his trade, none better, and soon became audible. His restraint commanded complete silence and especially riveted the attention of Mr. Balchin and Miss Wiseman, nor was it without effect on Mrs. Large. As for the Judge, he was used to it.

With the long tapering fingers of his left hand pressed firmly but gently upon the papers before him, his right making now and then the slightest of gestures to emphasize a point, the Great Advocate set forth with admirable lucidity the main lines of the affair.

A Parisian Master of the name of Bourrot (said Sir Anselm)—the Jury were well acquainted with that famous name — had left among other canvases of genius — alas! too few—one in particular which he deemed his *Masterpiece*. It represented that noblest of subjects for the inspiration of Genius, the Soul of that Middle Class, which is the backbone of every country; the painter's own, be it remembered, as well as ours. Unfortunately, for the world, the great Bourrot had died at a comparatively early age rather less than a year ago, which tragic event (Sir Anselm's voice remained firm throughout this passage, but was increasingly grave) gave very high value to the small number of canvases with which he had enriched the world. To none did it give higher value than to his *Masterpiece*, the "*Ame Bourgeoise*"—which term, as he need hardly inform them, was French for The Soul of the Middle Class. (Here most of the Jury, including Miss Wiseman, nodded, one—the horse-dealer—smiled cleverly, and the rest—but especially Mr. Balchin and Mrs. Large—looked solemn).

The Masterpiece came into the possession of our great Connoisseur in the Art World, Sir Henry Bensington, who patriotically exhibited it to the public in Bond Street before relegating it to his own famous collection, or selling it to some wealthy devotee of the

Muses, according as he might decide. And here let him add (Sir Anselm looked up at the Jury with a generous regard) that nothing should fall from him which could by one syllable suggest that Sir Henry, in all that followed, acted from any but the highest motives. He believed that Sir Henry was mistaken—nothing more.

While the Masterpiece was still being shown, his client, the Duke of Emonsillado, wrote to Sir Henry expressing his desire to buy, long before any other competitor entered the field. He begged the Jury to remember that point, and he emphasized it. Sir Henry replied that he had not yet decided whether he would or would not sell, but that he would bear the Duke's offer in mind. Immediately after—the Jury doubtless remembered the dreadful news which broke over England that fair spring morning — the picture disappeared! (Sir Anselm's voice sank to the profundity of mourning, and he remained silent for ten seconds with bowed head. Then, more briskly, he resumed.)

So far there was nothing under dispute. It was what followed that demanded their particular attention.

For some weeks there was no trace of the picture, and hope of its recovery had been abandoned. "At 6.45 p.m. on" (here Sir Anselm consulted his notes with exactitude) "yes, on Wednesday, the 13th of June, an individual appeared at the place of Mr. Gabriel of Cheyne Row (one whose acquaintance with modern French Art is larger and more intimate than that of any other man living), produced a small parcel, said that he was hard up, had a picture to sell, and asked five pounds for it. Mr. Gabriel on opening the parcel at once recognized the lost, the valuable canvas. He did his duty without hesitation to his profession, his distinguished colleague, his country and the civilized world. I shall call Mr. Gabriel," said Sir Anselm, "and you will be able to judge for yourselves his perfect loyalty and integrity, which I hope no one in this case disputes.

"First paying the sum required in order to get possession of the property, he bade his visitor wait while he put the parcel aside. He was not long doing so, but on turning round he discovered that the man had fled. He hastened to the door. The short street was deserted. Aged though he is, Mr. Gabriel ran to the corner, but no one corresponding to the stranger was visible.

"Mr. Gabriel's first act was to call immediately at Sir Henry Bensington's office to inform him (privately) that the picture was found. He was told that Sir Henry was travelling and would not be back for three days.

"Now I beg you to pay particular heed to what next happened. My Client, the Duke of Emonsillado, hearing of the discovery, was naturally anxious to judge for himself, and with the advice of experts, whether it was indeed the missing Masterpiece on the purchase of which he had already approached its owner. His

Grace has a wide experience of cultivated art in all its forms, and has for years shown the most acute judgment in the acquisition of his priceless collection at the Villa Emonsillado in Southern France. He is not a man to act precipitately. He waited till the next day to call on Mr. Gabriel, who knew him well as a distinguished patron of Art. They long inspected the picture together, and though no real doubt remained, the Duke was allowed to have it for a few hours in his suite at the Plantagenet Hotel, where certain friends and experts might see it.

"All was quite straightforward and indeed, if I understand aright, there is no complaint about this from the other side. Mr. Gabriel, who knew what a close friend the Duke was of Sir Henry Bensington's, wrote to him telling him all that had happened. His Grace gave a receipt; the canvas was to be returnable at a moment's notice, and he *at once* wrote himself to Sir Henry Bensington informing him of the loan, again offering to purchase (at the respectable figure of £20,000) and, of course, to hand the picture back immediately to its owner if sale was not intended.

"Then there happened that extraordinary series of events which has led to this case. Sir Henry on his return wrote genially to his old friend, my Client, assuring him that the picture (though he had not seen it!) was an obvious fake and worthless. That he was welcome to keep it. That the true original had turned up (how he did not say), and that he was sorry the Duke had been led into so palpable an error.

"His Grace would naturally have desired to see this strange *other* 'original.' That the picture he had the loan of was that same now familiar to all Europe he had not a shadow of doubt, nor had Mr. Gabriel, with his unique experience of such things. Dr. Edward Mowlem, curator of Oils in the Imperial Museum—by far our greatest expert—had confirmed what really should hardly need confirmation, and so had a host of others only less distinguished who had seen the canvas in the Duke's suite at the Plantagenet. But much as he desired to see the supposed rival, no opportunity was given him. The next thing he heard was that it had been purchased by the Marchioness of Norbolt, who publicly advertised her acquisition as authentic. My Client's legal advisers wrote to the Press respectfully pointing out her error. She only reiterated it, to the grave prejudice of the Duke's property (for he had now duly settled matters with Mr. Gabriel, though still willing — as he is a very wealthy man — to compensate Sir Henry Bensington).

"Under these circumstances my Client had no choice but to bring this action, and was astonished to hear that a counter-claim had been advanced. I shall call him, as also Mr. Gabriel and Dr. Mowlem, and when you have heard them there can be no doubt left in your minds."

The learned Counsel secretly conveyed to his mouth

a lozenge lovingly provided for him by Lady Utterleigh (like himself an Anglo-Catholic) and sat down—having spoken one hour and thirty-five minutes.

The first witness to be called was Mr. Gabriel. To Sir Anselm's plain questions he gave plain answers, setting forth the whole story, without the addition of any tedious detail such as the Duke's first payment of money. At the end, on the essential point of the picture's authenticity, he was quietly emphatic. Yes, he had the experience of a long lifetime, nearly all spent in purchases upon the Continent of modern pictures and especially of French. Sir Anselm brought out the fact that he had valued Bourrots for Sir Henry Bensington himself (whose name Mr. Gabriel pronounced with great respect). He had sold and resold examples of that master perhaps a hundred times. He was intimately acquainted with the "*Ame Bourgeoise.*" He had made a special study of it. There could be no manner of doubt that the Duke's copy was the original.

"No possible, probable manner of doubt. No shadow of doubt whatever!" suggested his Lordship, to the unaffected amusement of every lawyer in court over forty and the affected amusement of every lawyer under.

Sir Rory Hawlboy rose to cross-examine. His formidable figure alone might have struck terror into a soul less assured then Mr. Gabriel's. His frowning brow, his tauric skull, were adjuncts of victory. But if Sir Anselm was master of the Muted, Sir Rory was king of the Crescendo. He began on a note that, for him, was moderate, because, being a good tactician, he saw that Mr. Gabriel was not the weak point in the line. He reserved his loudest bawling for the decisive moment.

"Now, Mr. Gabriel," he said, not without a boom, but courteously enough, "you have told us that your mysterious visitor who brought the picture was with you for a few moments only."

"But five minutes."

"Oh! . . . but five minutes . . . now in five minutes had you the opportunity to observe him?"

"Not closely. He was a youngish man, dressed as I have described him, rather short, but with no distinctive characteristics."

"Ah! . . . No distinctive characteristics," and Sir Rory glanced at the Jury. . . . "May I ask whether it is your experience that youngish men, and rather short—no matter how dressed—generally come in with pictures worth many thousands of pounds and offer them to you for five?" Another glance at the Jury.

"If you mean that *Objets d'Art* are often offered at a fraction of their value, yes," answered Mr. Gabriel gently. "May I give instances, my Lord?"

Mr. Gabriel gave instance after instance from his own long career, but Sir Rory, who had hoped that this witness, like so many, would give an opportunity by overdoing it, was disappointed. The list was exact and overwhelming.

"Can you suggest why they act thus?"

"It is no part of my profession to discover that. I suppose that they are sometimes men who have found the thing by chance; often men who have played a receiver false."

"Then, Mr. Gabriel, was it not your duty to detain him and to inform the Police?"

"I have informed the Police. I intended to detain him when he took the opportunity as my back was turned to escape. It was my duty to secure Sir Henry's property, and I did so. I am profoundly glad that I did so."

"You are . . . profoundly . . . glad . . . Um! . . . And now, Mr. Gabriel, can you tell us precisely how and why you are so certain that the picture in the Duke's possession is the same as you saw and studied when it was on exhibition."

By way of answer Mr. Gabriel produced a mass of technicalities so exact, so numerous, so novel, so incomparable that the Jury were clearly moved. Sir Rory cut his losses.

"So it is your impression that this copy is the original?"

"Not my impression, sir, my unalterable opinion."

"Ah! Your *opinion*, Mr. Gabriel? Not your *conviction!*"

"Yes, my conviction. There can be no doubt of it."

"Well, Mr. Gabriel"—a look at the Jury—"we have had more than one expression . . . first it is your impression . . . then your impression becomes your opinion. Then it becomes your conviction, then that becomes unalterable . . . and so on. . . . I have nothing more to ask you, Mr. Gabriel."

Re-examination was superfluous.

And Mr. Gabriel stood down. His stock, already high, had risen thirty points.

After a few unimportant witnesses had given evidence on the arrival of the picture at the Plantagenet, the Duke of Emonsillado was called, and the name led to a general movement. All were eager to see in the flesh a man who had filled the papers for so long and who stood for such vast wealth. Mr. Balchin had expected a cloak and sombrero, Mrs. Large knee-breeches, buckles and a court sword, the letter-out-of-pleasure-boats a wizened yellow figure wearing orders, mustachiod and perhaps with a ruff round its neck.

In all this they were disappointed, but His Grace made a sufficient effect with his tall, spare figure and relentless features. He looked the part, if not of a Grandee, at least of a Pirate or Rover of the Spanish Main—which was all the same thing. And then, these millions would have carried off something much less striking.

Sir Anselm was a little nervous on beginning his examination of his witness, but his witness was not at all nervous under the Examination of Sir Anselm.

Sir Anselm had an instinctive dread of all that world to which Hardham belonged; but Hardham had no dread at all of lawyers in civil cases . . . only a lingering objection to Policemen, inherited from long past days, when he had been dealt with summarily. Sir Anselm feared that His Grace's manner and accent—though it was necessary to call him—might do his case harm. His Grace had no suspicion that he suffered in accent and manner, only a fine contempt for Pretty Fannies, the English accent and the damn drawl anyway.

Of all moods which affect the atmosphere of Human Converse, and can be felt pervading it before a word is spoken, Fear and its opposite are the strongest in effect. One could feel at thirty feet off the indifference of the tall, dark man in the box to wigs, legal mumbo-jumbo, the impeccability-of-lawyers myth and all the rest of the rubbish: Policemen were another matter. But Bench and Bar he mocked. He had millions and a tough constitution.

Moreover, Sir Anselm was in some dread of what the Duke's accent and manner might work on the Jury. He himself was so sensitive to anything savouring of the exceptional—the outer things—especially the things of Crown and Anchor, Double Cross, Morning Champagne, stale tobacco, so-dreadfully-coarse-ness, the unprintable, monkey-business and gee-gees, that he exaggerated the handicap. He didn't allow enough for the counter-weight of twelve millions and a title of romantic sonority.

And as a fact the Duke did very well. If his answers

were racy, they were clear, and the court was favourably impressed with him as a witness. He confirmed Gabriel's story exactly and added the details of his taking the canvas to the Plantagenet, of his letter to Bensington—whom he pleasantly called "Harry" every time—and of the visits of friends and experts (notably Dr. Mowlem of the Imperial Museum) to his rooms in the hotel. Was he prepared to reaffirm for the Jury his conviction that he possessed the original? Yep! He wuzz! He had long and particular acquaintance with Bourrot's work? Sure! Bourrot was his pet painter! Made a study of him for years. There could be no doubt of the identity between the picture exhibited at Martin's Rooms in the Spring and that which, from his strong box in the Plantagenet, had been conveyed to his bank? Naw! It wuzz key-stone. He'd lay Otto Kahn to a string o' Cowries.

Sir Rory opened his cross-examination more boldly than that of Gabriel, but still with the respect due to so great a fortune. He was loud and aggressive, but he didn't thunder—yet. He was keeping that for a better opportunity which he knew to be coming with another witness on whom he had information.

"Now, in the first place, your Grace, will you tell the Jury whether you have any suspicion of Sir Henry Bensington's good faith in this affair?"

"Harry? Harry's a white man!" Hands in coat pockets, grim but good-natured smile.

"Then how do you account for his contempt of what

you tell us is undeniably his own picture—a Masterpiece which he purchased at a high price and had studied more thoroughly than any man ? "

"Why, man, Harry's got to sell his stuff, ain't he ? "

"I suggest that you are virtually accusing Sir Henry Bensington of fraud ? "

"Then yer wrawng."

"What other interpretation can you place on his action ? "

"That's his funeral."

Here Mr. Justice Dove thought it necessary to intervene :

"I must interrupt a moment. I am not clear upon the exact *nuance* of your expression. How 'funeral' ? "

"Well, Lord, it's an old-fashioned expression, Ah 'llow, but Ah caught it young, tooting around among the boys. I mean it's Harry's own cabbage patch, his chicken-run, ye take me ? His very own li'l private back-yard, Huh ! His side of the split-rail-fence."

"You mean that you are not responsible for Sir Henry Bensington's judgment, that he is free to give his own explanation to the Court in due course, that you must confine yourself to what is of your own knowledge, and that you cannot testify to another man's motives or conclusions ? "

"Ye've said a lump, Lord," answered the Grandee with courteous acquiescence.

"Ah ! Now I think we have it clear ! " (To the Jury)

"The Duke intended to convey that he could only bear witness to matters within his own purview, and that he had no business with what he had not himself seen or heard. A very proper reservation."

Sir Rory Hawlboy changed front.

"You have told the Jury" (he waved a bit of paper in the air as though he were fumigating them) "that you have an intimate acquaintance with Bourrot's work?"

"Yep."

"Your experience of it is so minute and extensive that you can speak with authority?"

"Ah c'd tell a Bourrot with me eyes shet."

"Ah! With your eyes shut?" (A long turn to the Jury.)

"Yep! C'd tell a Bourrot in me sleep."

"In your sleep . . . ?" (More Jury ogling.) "Well, really, Duke, if your judgment of a picture is taken with your eyes closed and when you are asleep, I think the Jury needs nothing more to appreciate its value. They will draw their own conclusions."

There was no need to re-examine.

The Duke of Emonsillado stepped briskly out of the Box with the air of a man who could have carried on for hours.

A string of lesser witnesses followed, men who had in various degrees a claim to speak upon modern painting in general and Bourrot's rare works in particular. One of them, a Frenchman, was rather difficult to follow, from talking English with an Elizabethan vocabulary and a strange accent. Also, as he did not understand our procedure and rules of evidence, he so modified and qualified with a view to exact truth that, as a witness, he was detrimental. Sir Anselm got fidgety ; but he was relieved when the time came for the last and by far the most important name upon his list, and there was a craning of necks and movement throughout the Court when in loud tones the name of Dr. Mowlem was called.

CHAPTER XVIII

EDWARD MOWLEM was approaching his sixtieth year, and had increased in presence and volume of body, voice and learning from at least his eighteenth, when he had left an obscure secondary school in the West Riding for a scholarship at Fareham College in the more distinguished of the two ancient Universities.

As an undergraduate he had not been heard of, and was therefore free to study, took a very brilliant First, followed by a Research Fellowship and a year of intense study in Italy and France, devoted entirely to dear old Art. He returned with a reputation and a bundle of facts so considerable that he was already in the first rank of the profession on which he had determined. He was eagerly snapped up by the Civil Service, and after passing through a number of lesser posts, had been appointed, long before he was forty, to the Curatorship of Oils, English Furniture and Lace at the Imperial Museum. When English furniture had been erected to a separate department (in order to do something for poor Jenny's half-wit son Boko) Dr. Mowlem, as he now was, could devote himself entirely to his special subject. This, in the midst of a vast range of accurate knowledge throughout the whole field of Oil Painting, he had chosen in the special restricted limits of Modern French Symbolist Art.

On that nobody could touch him. He was a Corresponding Member of the principal foreign Societies, and was admitted as at least an equal even by the jealous and insular academic world of Paris. He was writing Bourrot's life, with access to all the documents. He had already published a lesser study immediately following on the Master's death, which was the admitted authority throughout England and America, North Germany, Australasia, and all the more progressive districts of the world, and which was not without a certain standing in Paris, little as that Capital can appreciate anything thorough and profound.

He was Sir Anselm's great gun — 17-inch, finely mounted for the occasion, loaded and prepared to deal devastation and death in the ranks of the opposite side. He appeared loaded with a pile of monstrous tomes, pamphlets and loose papers, including his own brochure on the Master, and bore on top of all André's large *Catalogue Raisonné*, which alone is sufficient to flatten all differing opinion to the earth.

As he grunted into the witness-box, shedding a book here and there, laboriously picking it up again and glaring through his huge spectacles at the paltry human beings about him, he gave the effect of a primeval Auroch, or monster Beeve of the Ukrainian Wild; and in contrast to Sir Anselm's first quiet question came a splendid roar of affirmation which bore down

Dr. Edward Mowlem, M.B.F.C., Curator of the Oil Paintings Department in the Imperial Museum, giving evidence in favour of the authenticity of the Duke of Emonsillado's Bourrot

upon the souls of the Jury like a sou'-westerly gale.

Hawlboy, hearing it, sniffed battle, and rejoiced to meet a foeman worthy of his lungs. What is more, that eminent King's Counsel smiled grimly, even ferociously, as he remembered what he held in reserve against this huge piece of ordnance.

The evidence in chief poured out in a mighty stream, through which Sir Anselm guided his craft with skill, though every moment in peril of swamping. It was a tornado of affirmation, thumped, clinched, devastating, supported by relay upon relay of document, quotation and example, stunning and destroying all doubt while it lasted; to say it convinced would be to use a word most miserably thin; it crushed, and, having crushed, recreated the formless mass into the aspect of an immovable creed.

But Sir Rory was not shaken. He had all ready, and was standing by.

He rose, I will not say in his majesty, for he was rather short, but in all his ponderous strength, and bull met bull. The Jury, already half deafened by the mighty protagonist of the Emonsillado Bourrot, were startled to discover the power which Sir Rory's larynx so suddenly developed.

He would have no nonsense; he would not be bullied; he would have the witness answer this, he would have the witness answer that; he would command the powerful animal to attention. It was a fine display of

Sir Rory Hawlboy reminding Dr. Mowlem that he is on his Oath

struggling horns locked in conflict, and for some time the battle hung even.

Already the cross-examination had done damage, learning had been caught contradicting itself on a date, making a slip of the tongue of a foreign name, and once had so far forgotten itself as to merit a rebuke from the Bench, when the consummate Advocate, filling his chest to what the Duke would have called capacity, lodged the unexpected and death-dealing blow.

"Now, Sir, listen to me! Chrm! You've told us, perhaps fifty times, that this canvas is with absolute certainty the original exhibited by Sir Henry Bensington —that canvas, on whose origin there is no dispute."

"I do! I have! Yes, I say again . . ."

"One moment!" Sir Rory's hand was uplifted in the gesture of a man who checks a plunging beast with a rein; his voice had suddenly changed. The Jury noted in it a quite new and restrained intensity. "Now, answer me this: *Have you ever set eyes on that original?*"

"On the Duke of Emonsillado's Bourrot."

"Don't trifle with the Court, Sir," bellowed his antagonist. "The original, I say the original! Have you ever set eyes on the original, either when it was exhibited in Bond Street, or in Sir Henry Bensington's place of business, or in its first home at North Merton, or anywhere else?"

There was an awful silence, during which the listeners might have heard a pin drop, and did as a fact hear a little squeak from Miss Wiseman.

"Now, Sir! Don't keep the Court waiting!"

The answer came muffled but still powerful.

"What of it?"

"Answer the question," said Mr. Justice Dove sharply.

Then that mighty voice replied, ah! manifestly wounded: "No, my Lord, I have not."

"Address your reply to Counsel," was His Lordship's order, adamantine and radamanthine for this occasion only—a manner most rare with him (unless, indeed, he were dealing with the discredited).

The stricken Monarch of the Herd faced his adversary: "No, Sir Rory," he said in a voice from the depths. "But I don't see . . ."

"You don't see!" thundered Sir Rory. "We don't want to hear what you don't see; we've just heard what you *didn't* see. You stand there, Sir, and you tell the Jury . . ."

"Of course I stand here," wailed the defeated man—if "wailing" be the term for the agony of a mighty storm; "where did you think I was?"

"That will do," bellowed Sir Rory; "that is enough, I think!" He swept the Jury with a commanding look, and then shot it like a furnace blast at the unhappy expert: "That is all, Sir!"

In vain did Sir Anselm try to redeem the situation by re-examining. It only made things worse, and he dropped it.

The vast form turned to descend from the elevation of its suffering, when the face which crowned it glanced round in turgid anger at the unmistakable sound of a snigger from the well of the Court. He glared in its direction, and saw there most unmistakably the short, very well dressed figure, the clean-shaven, firm, contemptuous face of his abominated rival expert, Archibald Dacy (whose mother was a Pimplehurst), the "expert"—the scented dabbler of the drawing-rooms, the fellow who hobnobbed with the ignoramus smart and bought and sold for them like a charlatan. He not only heard the snigger, he heard a whispered voice coming from those thin lips for the benefit of a neighbour :

"Reminds me of the Longworth business!"

It was an abominable blow! Once, once only had the immense learning of Mowlem been at fault, when he had advised the purchase for Longworth House of a Velasquez which turned out to have been painted eighteen months before in Marseilles. . . . That was twenty-five years ago. The great House had long forgiven him. He had remained its trusted adviser for two generations. . . . Oh! it was a felon thing to whisper that word "Longworth" while his soul was still bleeding! Luckily the two men were separated by a dense mass of crowded humans, but hatred poured through the air from the injured man to his insulter.

It can be guessed in what a triumphant mood Sir Rory Hawlboy rose to open his case, and in what full volume the booming voice charged forth to victory. He would not detain them long, nor did he; he pretended to no arts of persuasion or cajolement; he would call evidence ; he would deal with facts ; he had no fear of the consequence. When the Jury had heard the evidence of the only people with the least right to speak for the Masterpiece which they had themselves owned and intimately known, the one for years, the other in what was admittedly the best testing-place in Europe, the conclusion would be inevitable.

He would call Sir Henry Bensington, the one man in all the world best fitted to judge upon any such questions, and the only man, save the original owner, fitted to judge at all upon this one. He would call certain of Sir Henry's assistants, who would confirm the story of the recovery of the picture, but—and here he made an impressive pause—there was one he would call against whose unique value no criticism could stand. He referred to Mr. Delgairn himself, the original owner of the "*Ame Bourgeoise*." That gentleman, who they would remember (he wagged a stubby finger with vigour) had lived with the picture from boyhood, had studied it throughout his active and vigorous life, whose appreciation was necessarily worth more than all the rest of the world's put together, would swear to the authenticity of the Masterpiece which he himself had sold to Sir Henry, and which was now in the possession (Sir Rory reverently lowered his voice) of the great family of Walburton, and adorned, a priceless jewel, the richly-tapestried walls of Norbolt House.

The witnesses followed each other in well-chosen and telling succession. First came Henry Bensington, who, apart from his immense prestige, greatly impressed the

Court by the quiet, deep-rooted assurance and dignity in which he told his lucid and convincing story. His acquaintance with Bourrot, with the contract, the pains he'd been at to discover the whereabouts of the Masterpiece, his purchase of the same from Mr. Delgairn, how he had missed it when he had looked into his safe the day after the Exhibition had closed, how he had found it weeks after, lying in a neglected group of other picture parcels, how he had shown it to his assistants, and then had honourably disposed of it to its present owner, Lady Norbolt—at the mention of which name he slightly bowed.

Sir Anselm could not shake him in cross-examination ; there could of course be no question of anything but a misconception. How did he account for so strange a recovery ? Very simply ! We are often wrong in our recollection of automatic actions ; he had frequent occasion to put small canvases into the large safe, where there were usually a few put away. He had been fully under the impression that he had put the Bourrot there, but evidently he had been mistaken ; perhaps he had picked up another of similar size, for they must remember that these parcels were all made up and covered ; perhaps he had only intended to go to the safe and had not actually done so—at any rate, there could be no doubt at all of the recovery just where it might have been expected, among a number of other parcels which had been undisturbed for some time. Sir Anselm suggested that the canvas had been found

Refined but telling exposition of the Duke of Emonsillado's case by Sir Anselm Atterleigh

on the outside of the heap: not at all, it had been found in the middle, just where it would be if in the course of some weeks others had come in and had been laid against it. The whole thing was most sober, consistent, and conclusive.

It was the same thing with Sir Henry's two principal assistants, who followed, and who could not be shaken in cross-examination either upon any detail. They confirmed all that their principal had so quietly and effectively related; while they did so he never took his eyes from their faces.

Lastly, young Mr. Delgairn was put into the box and sworn, told the story of the purchase, with not a few irrelevances, but still understandably enough. It was evident he had a grievance against Sir Henry, and his testimony was only the more valuable. This grievance he kept dragging in, though more than once checked from the Bench. In particular, when he was quoting the sympathy of a neighbour of his, no less a public figure than General Sir Arthur Kenley, Mr. Justice Dove put the Court in a roar by a new and happy jest—"What the soldier said is not evidence," said the witty Judge—and all the Bar rocked with appreciative laughter.

Sir Henry Bensington's copy of the Bourrot (now Lady Norbolt's) was held up for the young man to judge, and he swore with a pained expression but emphatically that it was the picture he had lived with all his life, and which he could no more mistake than he could mistake any other familiar object of the old home.

Sir Anselm rose to cross-examine ; he was, if possible, more restrained than ever, and his voice was singularly mellow and telling, for he had just consumed another lozenge.

"You told us, Mr. Delgairn, that the picture which you have just identified is without any scintalla of doubt the picture you have known from boyhood : the original purchased by your late and universally lamented father."

The word "scintilla" is not a Squire's word, it is a legal term, and young Mr. Delgairn didn't know what it meant, but he plainly reaffirmed his absolute certainty.

"Very well," murmured Sir Anselm. He made a slight gesture, and a picture and frame were held up before the witness.

"Look at it carefully, Mr. Delgairn ; take your time ; we don't want to hurry or confuse you."

While the young man was contemplating the Masterpiece, Sir Anselm Atterleigh was pursuing that favourite occupation of his tribe, casting "the tender long regard" upon the Jury ; his eyes were saying, in a fashion more refined than mine, "Just you wait, my Pippins ! There's going to be a surprise for you ! "

After a good long interval—not too long to dull the effect—he turned to his victim and asked kindly :

"You are quite satisfied, Mr. Delgairn ? "

"Quite, Sir." The voice was firm and utterly decided.

"*That*" (Sir Anselm's voice slightly rose in volume) "is without a doubt the picture with which you have lived all these years, and to which you can swear with full confidence?"

"It is."

Sir Anselm's voice lowered again, but became a little staccato and more distinct than ever.

"Would it surprise you to learn, Mr. Delgairn, that this picture to which you have sworn is *not* the original which you identified for the jury a moment ago? It is not Lady Norbolt's copy—it is the Duke's."

Sensation.

"Hold them both up," said Sir Anselm.

The twin canvases were held up side by side before the eyes of the astonished young man.

"I don't . . ." he gasped.

"That will do, I think," said Sir Anselm, toying with his watch-chain, and the cross-examination was at an end.

Sir Rory wisely refrained from re-examining. But in a loud mutter he consigned all squires to Hell.

Only one witness remained, and after such a scene he was something of an anti-climax. Archibald Dacy planted his short and sturdy but fine figure before Judge and Jury, and swore to his quite unshaken judgment. The picture which he had seen on twenty occasions, on its purchase, on exhibition, and privately in Norbolt House, was indubitably the same as he had had the privilege of studying when first it had appeared in London. His cross-examination was perfunctory,

Astonishment of young Mr. Delgairn to find that he has committed perjury, which is Foul Bad Form: what?

but in the course of it he dropped a remark which was to bear fruit. In tones which for coolness and acidity recalled a lemon ice, he cut to the bone the absurdity of Dr. Mowlem, and managed to slip in that damnable but damning reference to the fearful *gaffe* at Longworth.

Sir Rory Hawlboy covered his retreat magnificently, depending almost entirely upon his artillery; his shouts and trumpetings, booms, roars and bellows, his purple face, tempestuous wig, windmill of a right arm and hammer of a fist, working all out in full blast, did in some degree obliterate the vision of poor Delgairn stammering and staring at those miraculous, those diabolic doubles.

He made great play with the absurd confession of Dr. Mowlem and turned the knife anew in the deep wound, until the great expert was one mass of rage, further inflamed by the contemptuous glance of the rival Archibald.

Sir Anselm concluded effectively just at the right length in the most lucid order, and it remained for the Court to decide.

Mr. Justice Dove first ordered the Jury to make careful examination of either canvas, and it was a fine example of that legal system which we have carried to the highest perfection known to man, to see the General Grocer in a good way of business, the Letter-out-of-pleasure-boats on the Thames, Miss Wiseman (who had read many works of fiction), the Horse-dealer, Mrs. Large, and the rest, scrutinizing with critical eye the disputed work of the French Symbolist School in what

Superb and triumphant indignation of Sir Rory Hawlboy in defence of Lady Norbolt's case

Deliberation of Miss Althea Wiseman, jury-woman, on a masterpiece

presumably must have been, in one case at least, its supreme achievement; and even in the other an admirable copy.

Mr. Balchin plumbed the depths of a composition the enigma of which might have intrigued a lesser mind, Mrs. Large took a matron's sweeping grasp of the problem, the Letter-out-of-houseboats lingered affectionately first upon the one then upon the other, the Horse-dealer first upon the other then upon the one; both showed in their features the spell that genius can cast and the power of pictorial art at its greatest over the human soul.

As for Miss Wiseman, she almost tried the patience of the Judge by her minute, her loving exploration of all those depths beyond depths which the inspired brush of Bourrot could reveal.

When the twelve good bisexual specimens of humanity and true had had their fill of æsthetic nourishment and critical contemplation, Mr. Justice Dove proceeded to the summing up.

That master of our Common Law marshalled the evidence with that genius which—by a happy coincidence all judges whatsoever have possessed—at least within living memory. He disentangled the relevant from the irrelevant; he showed with benign patience how much might be said upon the one hand, leaning somewhat to the right as he did so and accompanying that part of his survey with a broad movement of the right arm; he then most impartially

Mr. Justice Dove showing all there is upon the one side

Mr. Justice Dove showing all there is upon the other side

showed how much might be said upon the other hand, leaning somewhat to the left as he did so, and accompanying this second portion with a movement equally broad of the corresponding limb. He did not disdain to decorate the necessarily lengthy oration with flowers of humour and flashes of eloquence ; he admitted towards its close one of those panegyrics upon his own corporation and all connected with it, which are at once so well deserved and so necessarily a part of our happy Commonwealth.

He concluded by submitting to the Jury (who by the way, he reminded, were there to judge facts, not law) the following six points :—

1. Had Lady Norbolt good and sufficient reason to think her copy the original ?

2. Did she act maliciously when she denounced the rival copy to be a fraud ?

3. Had she suffered damage by the pretensions put forward for his copy by the Duke of Emonsillado ? If so, in what amount ?

4. Had the Duke of Emonsillado good and sufficient reason to think his copy the original ?

5. Did he act maliciously when he denounced the rival copy to be a fraud ?

6. Had he suffered damage by the pretensions put forward for her copy by Lady Norbolt ? If so, in what amount ?

The Jury retired.

The time during which a Jury is deliberating is

commonly one of a certain boredom in Court. There is nothing to occupy the attention. But this memorable occasion was an exception.

Archibald Dacy sauntered out to smoke a cigarette. That cigarette was never smoked. He was followed with stealthy, ursuline step by the monstrous Mowlem, and hardly were they both outside the door in the public passage when the Mountain of Learning fell with howls of rage upon the Darling of the Drawing-rooms.

It was the Imperial Official who got in the first blow. But the Dude parried the second and countered with a fine straight body blow above the heart, under which the heavy-weight reeled. The Doctor returned to the charge, and began to do some very damaging work, clipping from the left, as excited steps rang along the Spanish Arches of the Law Courts, and the crowd about the combatants gathered in volume. Bets began to be laid, and favourites chosen, as the two Elders, the Big 'un and the Bantam, warmed to their work.

Blood will tell! And Archibald Dacy (whose mother was a Pimplehurst) landed the Learned One a biff in the left optic just as that Museumite was about to score a foul by crushing his opponent's head with a copy of André's *Catalogue Raisonné*. A biff in the left optic, I say, and put it out of action. So much for the Middle Classes!

The Curator crumpled up, nursing his injured Peeper, and roaring like a Cyclops. Archibald triumphed so openly between puffs that the gigantic Civil Servant,

Altercation between two Experts on Modern Art, the one Academic, the other on a Higher Plane

for all his suffering, lashed out a vicious kick; but even as it took effect two policemen, who ought to have been there long before, clove the crowd, separated the experts by the scruff of their necks, and lugged them, violently protesting, away.

Meanwhile, in Court, the Jury had returned. The thunder and the shouting having now died in the corridor outside, and the warriors forcibly departed, it was in complete silence that questions were put to Mr. Balchin, Foreman of the Jury, when that body had returned and filed into its place.

1. Had Lady Norbolt good and sufficient reason to think her copy the original?

Yes. The Jury decided that she had.

2. Did she act maliciously when she denounced the rival copy to be a fraud?

Yes, she did.

3. Had she suffered damage by the pretensions put forward for his copy by the Duke of Emonsillado? If so, in what amount?

Yes, she had: in the amount of Twenty thousand pounds.

4. Had the Duke of Emonsillado good and sufficient reason for thinking his copy to be the original?

Yes, he had.

5. Did he act maliciously when he denounced the rival copy to be a fraud?

Yes, he did.

6. Had he suffered damage for the pretensions put

forward for her copy by Lady Norbolt? If so, in what amount?

Yes, he had: in the amount of Twenty thousand pounds.

Mr. Justice Dove complimented the Jury on their answers, with which he thoroughly agreed, and costs would of course be divided.

CHAPTER XIX

YOU will have noticed (Lady deigning to read this book) that even during the brief bright years which have passed between your girlhood and your present young matronly days, human life was not chaotic, but followed so regular a plan that one might almost fall into the superstition of a Providence.

The only man I know at all intimately who has denied this divine purpose in human life is William Shakespeare, but I do not think he really doubted it: after all, he only put it into the mouth of one of his characters, a weak fellow who was egged on by his wife to murder people, and whose nerves and judgment went all to pieces as a consequence. No: things *do* work out on a pattern, and very odd it is. There seem to be no loose ends.

Therefore may you confidently expect that two "*Ames Bourgeoises*," each claiming to be the veritable and authentic and original "*Ame Bourgeoise*," and neither being demonstrably the authentic and original, etc., would not be allowed (I use the word in no anthropomorphic sense) to knock about this world at random, like two barges which have broken moorings in a gale on the Lower Thames. A solution was bound to arrive. For if it had not, how should the universe be rational at all? And the solution did arrive, by one of those accidents which impious men might call coincidence, but to which the wise give a nobler name.

First let me call to your attention a phenomenon which I am sure had not come within your personal experience, but which is vouched for by the distinguished author of "*Alcohol and Human Organismic Synthesis*" (a woman of European fame), Mrs. Whortleberry.

The phenomenon is this: A little drink (though it may not be true that it won't do us any harm) quickens the faculties of perception: a lot dulls them. Indeed, a very great deal may result in complete oblivion. (As we know from the case of Sir Charles Gaddy, during the debate on the Indian Balances.) In a notable experiment, when twelve separate doses ranging from a single cubic centimetre to twenty-two were tried on twelve midinettes . . . but, really, I can't go on like this, I must get to business.

And what I was coming to, anyway, was that Mr. Chas. Goatcher, the forlorn, the unfortunate, the exiled Mr. Goatcher, coming now after so many days and weeks to the end of his resources (careful as he had been, regularly as he had taken advantage of the summer weather to enjoy by night the pleasant air of the Thames Embankment, abstemious as he had been—in food—reserving such few pence as he dared spend for his daily and more necessary consumption) was to prove a living example of the truths about Alcohol which I have just been putting to you at such intolerable length.

It will be remembered that this distressed citizen had on the fatal night when the lost Masterpiece became really lost visited not more than three public-houses, which is far from a record.

Therefore it was that the aspect of The Butcher's Arms with its glaring red front and plate glass under the arc light had etched itself into that part of his mind which sinks below the level of the conscious (have I got it right ?) to rise again when it feels inclined for a breather.

Much of what had happened after he had passed the portals of The Butcher's Arms was confused, and the last of the episode, as he had staggered into bed, was lost ; but the glaring red paint and the plate glass and the name under the arc lamp lay there moored like a mine not a fathom below the surface, and ready to pop up and explode from the sub-liminal (Oh, blessed word ! —How these words do chase one another ! I wish I knew the modern one—I am using the mumbo-jumbo of my youth) from the sub-liminal, I say, and spring out when it might least be expected—" on contact."

That contact came one night when, as I have told you, poor Mr. Goatcher was reaching the very end of his resources ; when he had but half-a-crown left. He was slouching round the corner of a street, in the wrong part of town, when he blundered upon The Butcher's Arms —and it all came back to him like the boomerang in the lying travel books of our childhood.

There it was! There was the place whence the "*Ame Bourgeoise*" had been snatched away by some unscrupulous scoundrel, in the pursuit of whom he had fallen and covered himself with blood, shame and disaster.

In spite of such unpleasing associations, he went in. After all, it was the nearest pub. It was time for his third go, and he still had half-a-crown.

When he got into the bar he felt an odd sensation as though he had missed something from under his arm. Had he not been carrying something? No, it was the effect of the similar surroundings and the recollection of the fatal night.

The door between the bar and the Snuggery wherein reigned the lord of that hostelry was open. And there in his majesty he sat, entertaining two intimate friends, in his shirt-sleeves as was his wont, and having above him "*Stiggins's Nightmare*," better known to a wealthier and more parasitic world as the Masterpiece of the Immortal Bourrot.

For when Mr. Goatcher had left the Bourrot by alcoholic inadvertence in this hostelry, the daughter (and Barmaid) of the House had found it and carried it to her Sire. Who, frowning, gave it this title of "*Stiggins's Nightmare*," and put it up in his Snuggery as a warning to all teetotallers.

Mr. Chas. Goatcher did not always trust himself at the beginning of a third go. He did not rub his eyes, because no one ever does do that unless they have got something into them; but he stared. He did not

The Bourgeois Soul in Two Examples (being the landlord of The Butcher's Arms depicted in photographic art sitting beneath an adornment of his Snuggery)

pinch himself, because that would have hurt . . . but he slowly, and, I am afraid, rather drunkenly, verified (as they say in the Universities) the object before him. Then he said, a little too thickly, to the young lady who had originally rescued the priceless thing:

"Could I speak to the Guv'nor a minute?"

She looked at him with a proper disdain, priced the squalor into which his recent dereliction had sunk him, and asked him what he wanted.

"Tell the Guv'nor," he whispered hoarsely, "that I can make it worth his while about that picture," and he butted his head vaguely forward. She turned to see what he meant.

"Oh, that!" said the daughter of the house. "Father's very fond of that."

"Well he may be!" said Mr. Goatcher mysteriously. Then with an unfortunate hesitation, due to his failing, he added the remarkable words, "I could find him ten pounds for it!"

"When I see it!" replied the maiden calmly. "Now then: you've had enough." And she refused to serve him again.

More sobered by the shock of revelation than by the balm of a woman's voice, Mr. Charles Goatcher grasped what he had to do. It was rather like the way in which a man grasps a lamp-post on critical occasions, but still, he grasped the business in hand.

He thanked Heaven (for he had a simple mind, and believed in Heaven as the unfortunate will) that there were still some few pence left in his poor pocket. He dropped two of them into the slot of a telephone box near at hand, and after getting the wrong number twice, heard Henry Bensington's voice at the other end of the wire.

He heard a mixture of astonishment and anger; then an eager attention. He felt that for so great a service he was forgiven. He gave the name of the public-house, of the street; he humbly accepted an appointment for the morning of the following day, not at the King Street office, but at a certain rendezvous in a workman's coffee-house which both he and his master had used before.

* * * * *

A little more than half an hour after Mr. Goatcher had slunk off to what would be the last of his nights of fasting and bedless misery, Henry Bensington, quietly dressed, but with plenty of the marks of wealth about him—not only in his gestures and manner of speech but in the details of his clothing—drew up at The Butcher's Arms, not in a car, but in a taxi—a sufficient sign of grandeur in such a neighbourhood. He was respectfully received. And the astonished lady discovered (let us hope she remembered the lesson!) that drunken men sometimes tell the truth. Evidently a message had been sent, and here was a Gentleman—there was no mistaking that!—who was asking quietly whether he might see the proprietor. He had an offer to make for a certain picture.

The Master of The Butcher's Arms, on hearing the news, slipped on his coat, touched his hair with a greasy little brush kept upon a shelf for the purpose, and entered into negotiation. Nor did that negotiation take long, for the words "Ten pounds" had already been used to his own knowledge, from his daughter. Bensington wisely proffered fifteen—and in cash, of course.

Henry Bensington (as may be imagined from what has already been seen of his ability in such affairs) did not omit to hint that the property must have been come by in some dubious fashion.

The whole thing was over in ten minutes, while the taxi waited. The owner of The Butcher's Arms had stuffed fifteen well-worn notes into his waistcoat-pocket (not consecutive—no chance of tracing) and the original, the authentic, the indubitable "*Ame Bourgeoise*" was rolling back tightly clasped under the firm arm of Henry Bensington, as its little brothers had been in those of his fellow picture-dealers Caen and Alessandria, whom he had defeated in battle and whose scalps adorned his walls.

Such are the masters of this earth.

* * * * *

It was a half-hour's drive back to his office (all had been shut there long ago when he let himself in), and already he knew what was to be done—it was the last (please the pigs!) of these interminable machinations. He had manœuvred all his life, and tricks had made him a millionaire; but one can have too much of a good thing. Really the twisting and untwisting of these last few months was enough to make the strongest head giddy!

The next morning he met Mr. Goatcher in the workmen's coffee-house, took that worthy to a slop-shop and rigged him out, bore him back to the office, sternly ordered him to an upper room where he was to remain attendant till he might be called for, and then he himself sat down to write what surely would be the last note of all those notes, to his Grace the Duque de Emonsillado.

It was more than a note—it was a letter; a long letter, carefully worded and in parts almost eloquent.

It informed the Duke that against all expectation there had been found what might be—Bensington could not swear to it—the original of what had caused so much contention and, alas! such a great expenditure of money—no one regretted the contention or the expenditure of money more than did the writer.

In so far as he might be the cause of such worries he, Bensington, apologized fully; but the startling fact was there, and there was no getting out of it. One of the emissaries whom he had sent to search for the picture when it was lost—and who of course had failed to find it—had returned that very day, that very morning. He had come upon this copy suddenly in a public-house in a poor part of the town. Whether the explanation given of how it got there were true or not Bensington could not say; he could only take the word of the owner, who was willing to part with it quite readily and assured him that it had been left in the bar one day by accident. Bensington presumed that the thief had drunk too much and had left it behind him, and dared not return to take possession. The publican had used it as an ornament to his private room, showing it to one or two friends, and it was there, through conversation, that his agent had learned of it. If Hardy thought the clue insufficient he could do nothing more. It might be worth his while to purchase in order to end these bewildering confusions. If he would come round, his agent would tell him the whole story and he should decide.

In due course the Duke came round: but in a forbidding mood. He was getting tired of the procession. He had had a meal of the thing :—to the back teeth.

He listened carefully to Mr. Goatcher's tale, how he had sought high and low for Sir Henry's lost canvas, how a clue had been afforded him through a gentleman's conversation, and how he had discovered the Masterpiece in a public-house near Seven Dials. Hardham listened with the same hard and unchanging eye to the arguments in favour of this last of the claimants—how it had all the appearance of stolen goods abandoned, and how it would not have been in such a place were it not of that character—and so on and so on.

He was taking none.

"D'ye read the noospapers, Mr. Whatcher-may-call-um ?" said the Grandee to the earnest pleader for art.

The Duke of Emonsillado (and the rest) estimating what elements of truth there may be in a Business Proposition

"Why?" asked Mr. Goatcher humbly.

"'Cawse if ye' do, it seems strange ye' went on looking for that there picture—after they'd given thet Solomon's judgment and divided the child in court, eh? Aw! Come off!"

The Duke of Emonsillado rose at the end of this conference, stretched his arms and legs rather vulgarly, shook Sir Henry warmly by the hand, assured him that it was all N.G., winked, and was off.

Another man than Bensington might have abandoned the chase. After all, he had touched a solid twenty thousand pounds, and there was nothing easier than to burn what he now knew well to be the authentic and original, etc., etc. But it is the just boast of such men that they suck the last drop out of the orange of this world before proceeding to another which they forbear to contemplate. He sat down at once and wrote to Lady Norbolt:

"My dear Lady Norbolt,

"The matter of this may astonish you—I hope it will not alarm you. You can test for yourself anything I say in it: and you will find that I am telling the truth. A few hours ago an agent of mine who has served me faithfully for many years and whom I have never known to fail me, telephoned to me that he had come upon what he fully believed to be the original '*Ame Bourgeoise*.'

"Pray read on. I have told you the worst at once.

"He was led to it by the clue of a chance conversation in one of the poorer parts of London. He found it hung on the walls of a publican's private room, where it had been ever since it was left (apparently) by the thief in drunken inadvertence all those months ago. I obtained it without difficulty. I have it here with me in my room.

"Now I cannot pretend that this is indeed the original, and that the copy which you have is something other. Your copy may be a replica made by Bourrot (as I personally should believe) or, in some other inexplicable way, so resembling the original as to be confused with it. Or it may indeed be the original and what I have here may be something Bourrot did himself by way of replica, or in some other way was produced.

"It is my duty to tell you that the Duke of Emonsillado, whose confidence in his undoubtedly valueless copy may have been shaken by my considered evidence in court, has come to my office in connection with this new discovery, but has not yet made any firm offer; and I think it therefore all the more my duty to tell you the whole transaction, and to give you the option of purchase.

"I ought not perhaps to take less than I honestly believe I could obtain from anyone of a dozen competitors; seeing the doubt which now hangs over both canvases, that which I sold you, and that which has just reached me. But since, though there is no legal obligation, I feel myself bound in honour to consider your difficulty, I am prepared to let you have it and take it immediately from my office where it lies before me for a sum not more than that which I received for the example at present in Norbolt House. I do not know whether the presence of yet another competing candidate for the title of Bourrot's original Masterpiece will give you any anxiety. It should not do so if you are convinced of the unique character of your own.

"I leave the decision to you; but I would like an answer at the earliest possible moment, and it would certainly be best for you to come here privately and see the picture with me."

* * * * *

Verecundia, Lady Norbolt, came round. She was very angry but calm. She told Bensington plainly that he had caught her and that it was abominable. He kept his temper and pointed out, quite reasonably, that she wasn't bound to buy. His price was, of course, the old one: twenty thousand. If she liked to leave it knocking about, with all sorts of discussions and articles on it—well . . . and he shrugged his shoulders.

Verecundia, Lady Norbolt, told him a number of home truths which he listened to patiently.

Then she paid.

CHAPTER XX

Two of this bewildering trinity were in the hands of the persistent woman. The third, the one the Duke held, was out of reach—but at any rate, there was no other competition, or, if any appeared—well, then, to hell with everything!

Meanwhile everyone must use his weapons and Verecundia's weapon was The World. There she had Hardy in a lead pipe clinch! *He* wasn't accepted. *She* could buy all London and make it come to Norbolt House.

She would give a grand evening with the Masterpiece—the original, the authentic, the pure and blushful—displayed, and a lecture thereon and the whole bag of tricks. That would settle things for ever—as far as they could be settled in such an unimagined welter of forgeries!

* * * * *

The great day was at hand. The solemn pageant and triumph of the veritable, the unquestionable, the final "*Ame Bourgeoise*" was to be made manifest to all men in the largest room, the ballroom, of that great Palace modestly entitled "Norbolt House." There were only two clear days to run, but there was yet one essential to be decided. Who should they get to Pontificate? To proclaim the Idol? To shroud it in the necessary clouds of incense if their mainstay failed? They had trained all their guns on Vavassour—but Vavassour had remained as silent as brazen fates.

Vavassour was the obvious man. What he said not only went but galloped and charged. It confirmed and established. He was the one man in England to whose judgment universal opinion bowed in all that concerned modern art.

How he had obtained his reputation puzzled the simple. It doesn't puzzle me.

He had done it by the exercise of three rules, two positive and one negative.

His first rule was to write and talk upon Art with words no one else had ever heard of in such a connection. Some he had imported. Some he had invented. Most of them were quite ordinary little English adjectives and nouns which could have no conceivable relation to sculpture or painting or anything of the kind. Thus in a short but stupendous appreciation of Williams' Headless Horse (which, through Vavassour's article was chosen for the Triumphal Arch on the new Charing Cross bridge) he had called it, among other things, "monosyllabic." "Captrous like so much Turkish work, or at any rate Bessarabian," "*lointain*" and "*gebraunt.*" Also "a diminished seventh" and "tapped."

The second rule was to hammer and to hammer and to hammer persistently. He talked and he wrote and he lectured, and he brought out little books and prefaces and pamphlets and epigrams and private judgments and public pronouncements and after-dinner orations without a break, taking the greatest possible care to pay no attention to anything whatsoever except dear old Art.

Those were his two positive rules of conduct whereby he had accumulated, though still well under forty, a very comfortable little fortune, purchasing therewith a house at Putney. From the garden gate of this he would commune with the Immensities, feeding upon solitude, and resolutely refusing himself to all beggars, tramps, autograph hunters and millionaires. There he wrote, thence he proceeded (at a proper fee) to give a lecture or a speech or the glory of his presence at a private feast.

And his third, negative, rule was this; never to buy or sell any object of Art whether on his own account or for other people; and never by so much as a pencil scratch to attempt any work of his own.

In this last resolution he was powerfully aided by nature and by nature's God, who, between them, had deprived him of all artistic capacity whatsoever. He couldn't draw an egg—and that alone put him far above the masters of our time, who can all of them, somehow, turn out something, though they themselves have no idea what it be.

Such was Vavassour. You must excuse my lingering upon him. He fascinates me.

Verecundia had written to him days ago. She had learned the largest fee he had ever got (what dear Nellie had paid him only last month to dine with her). She had doubled it and put the cheque in her letter—but she got no answer, and she was getting anxious!

"He's so difficult to get at," she sighed to Ardee and Elless amid a mountain of invitation cards and plans and answers and bills and orders. "He won't have his name in the telephone book, and he lives at Putney."

"Well, Putney's not so far off," snapped Elless, who had a decayed Aunt in that delightful suburb.

"No, but one can't go all that way on chance," said Ardee.

"Ah cer'nly thought that cheque 'ud land him," continued the Noble Widow in a grieved voice, "he can't have wannted *more*."

"Oh, he'll come all right," said Elless, and Ardee brilliantly intervened with the murmur that he was like everybody with an artistic temperament.

Elless was right as usual. There is nothing like poverty to sharpen the judgment, and even as she was opening her ferret trap of a mouth to make another comment on the fruitful avarice of all Putneyites the telephone bell rang, and Verecundia was overjoyed to hear the voice of her Major Domo respectfully announcing that Mr. Vavassour wished to speak to her.

Meditations of Genius at Putney

The high-bred restraint of that great lady's features was relaxed in twenty ways during the short conversation that followed as she sat leaning forward in rapture with the instrument glued to her ear.

"Is that you, *dear* Muster Vavvasour ?"

But there was no mistaking the dreamy, soft, inspired voice which replied. Verecundia's eyes registered admiration and ecstacy. "What, ye've been sick ?" Her brows expressed pathos and alarm.

"Oh, *not* the throat ; the Big Toe. Which foot ?" The handsome mask passed from relief to sisterly regard.

"What, crushed ?" Horror.

"But all right now ?" courteous inquiry.

"Oh, yeh *can* come." Fatuous glory. "Oh, thank yeh, dear Mr. Vavvasour, thank yeh ! Oh, no . . . Ah'll send one of the cars," generous patronage (which shows itself principally in the corners of the mouth).

"They all tell me it doan matter being at night. . . . Yes, we've got that new light. . . . What, it doesn't matter with symbolism what hour it is. . . . ?" Puzzlement. "Exactly ! and it is so difficult to get the men during the day now that everybody is in the City."

"Thank yeh again, oh, so much ! . . . then the car Thursday at your house at nine. We begin at ten." Final registration of decision, and general winding-up-ed-ness. Another deep sigh of achievement and satisfaction, and the receiver was clicked up again.

The last lists were read over, the names checked, the big plan of the chairs and platform carefully scrutinized and the place for Royalty in the front row marked with a little red cross.

And now for two days on intensive press work, and then action!

* * * * *

It was a fine crush and it did honour to Verecundia's twenty millions. "Pig" Hamilton was there from the word go. The Barltons came early, which was a great favour, and both Bidderlings, the Indian ones and the one at the Treasury, and Dolly brought Jane with him as well, who was presented to the Royalties with some form, and George came too. Then there was Bailey Pott, and Harry Crutch and "Horse," who was really grateful to Verecundia, because she had paid for his step up in the peerage, and he did anything she asked him, though he couldn't stick these painting and writing fellahs (what?), and Ganzer the new attaché and Morino who hardly went anywhere — and his hostess's eyes beamed at the sight of him; Worsebeach and Jaggers and his wife and her friend Jack Poole, and Kinky Beale—who was tight and tried not to show it—and Pirry who had just bought Sir Edward (out of Morning Star by Fancy That; and a wise speculation it was, for he was showing finely and the odds were hardening like glue). Poor old Lord Gunter came, and that was really kind of him. Yes! Verecundia meant it! Most of them thought he was dead. He must have made a great effort. The Prime Minister was somewhere about, but he was difficult to spot in such a crowd and not worth worrying about, anyhow; but Lady Sharp was another matter, and Verecundia pushed through to congratulate her loudly on the Election, and her little husband beamed. The Duke of St. Ives was specially welcome. He really *had* come to do honour to Bourrot's name, Verecundia said; and he was so keen on it that he had brought Peach with him, and Verecundia was quite kind to her for a minute and so was Archie, but the Duke didn't like it and Polly captured him—which was wise of her, for the Duke made scenes sometimes. then there was Mrs. Roebeck and Anna Bogles with her eyeglass and of *course* Gaby Wyoming, with two other film stars whose names I forget, and old Buster.

But I mustn't trouble you with any more of their names—you know them all. London's a small place. Dear Archibald was there, of course; but the Curator wasn't because he hadn't been asked. Besides which, Elless had reported, after due research, that the old boy still had a black eye. It's astonishing how long they take to heal after sixty. Monsieur Caen and Signor Alessandria were in great form. They had asked themselves. They found it always worked, and Verecundia was deeply impressed when Archibald had taken her aside and told her that Monsieur Caen was the greatest expert on Bourrot in France, but still more so when Lady Sharp had told her later that Signor Alessandria had no equal in Italy. So Monsieur Caen and Signor Alessandria were given places of honour in the second row, behind the Royalty, when the audience was marshalled to its chairs in the crowded ballroom.

The thing had been done with all Lady Norbolt's energy and thoroughness. She had grasped Henry Bensington's colour scheme and reproduced it tenfold. The whole place was hung in black, covering windows and all the walls so amply as to fall in rich folds of heavy unreflecting velvet and trail by a foot and more upon the floor, the waxed parquet of which was lost under a black carpet of a pile as soft and deep as a mother's love or the lowing of far kine at evening. And all the chairs were black.

At the end of the room, with a broad gangway between it and the first row of chairs (where the Royalty was) rose a platform, from wall to wall, carpeted black, draped black and with a row of little shaded lamps at the edge, like foot-lights: curtains as black on all sides. In the midst was a table draped in black; and at the back, alone, like a god to be worshipped, hung the Masterpiece. Up on to that platform by a little black bench at the side stepped Verecundia. She bowed slightly (as the fashion now was) to the Royalty and then gave tongue in her luminous contralto.

"Ah'm not going to give yeh anny word to keep yeh from the vurry high privilege we have of hearing the greatest jedgment that can be given by the greatest of living ap-preciative genius upon the greatest dead genius of form and colour and ideea:— Mr. Vavvasour."

She gave a snap-shutter glance to her left, made an

imperceptible gesture with her left hand, popped down into the audience again into the chair next the Royalty. There was an impressive interval—just long enough—and from a hidden overlap of curtain to the side of the stage—The Vavassour glided on.

He leant in nonchalance, inspired, against the table, his left elbow reposing thereon, his right hand grasping twice at the air, his noble head bowed. Then, slowly, he raised those Attic features and fixed his gaze, abstracted, at a point in the N.E. by E. in traverse, and at thirty-seven degrees elevation, as though caught by some starry influence. He lifted that sensitive right hand and ran its delicate diaphanous fingers through his Ambrosian hair; and still that mighty silence.

A whisper came from the midst of that hushed audience; it was Anna Bogles. "He's going to be sick!" she said, and too many people heard her. But genius was rapt in vision. Then the lips spake: a low but intense, a carrying musical message: one word . . . "Bourrot". . . . Then again there was silence for at least a minute and a half, which felt like half an hour, and was meant to.

Then in lower, much lower, vibrating triumphant tones—once more the name of Power . . . "Bourrot . . . !" . . . and once more silence.

The audience sat as still as death, except for old Lord Gunter who coughed horribly and began shouting, "Oh! Dear! Oh! Dear!" until Peach who was just

Genius inspired to Utterance of the Word by the Presence of Rank and Fashion

behind him, slapped him hard on the back and whispered, "Shut up, you old fool!" whereat once more mysterious silence reigned. It reigned about another minute and a half, during which you might have heard your own conscience, and then for the third time came the awful summons—but this time from a clarion; there was no doubt but Vavassour had a range of notes—and once more, imperatively this time, the imperial name—"*BOURROT!*" . . . What shall we say" (the voice sank, the head drooped) "of *Bourrot* . . . What of the dead, the vanished. . . . Ah! Humanity, Promethean, doomed, indefatigable, unconquered . . . is Bourrot dead?"

More silence. Mr. Vavassour dropped his head (with its chin) allowed his hair to flop over his forehead, hung his hands helpless before him and sobbed. "Yes! . . . Bourrot is dead!"

Silence number four, and this time unbroken, except for Gaby Wyoming's understudy, who was crying gently and murmuring: "Oh! ain't he wonnerful!"

"Bourrot is dead"—the Master raised himself to his full height. "Dead? . . . and yet, not dead! . . ." The master swung round and pointed with a prophetic, rigid arm to the Masterpiece. . . . "That eye, that beam Luciferan, that counter-stroke with its corrugated shaft of vengeance—all which is before us in the unmatchable symbolism of Hate, pierces our sleeping souls and wakes them to Haro! against the Bourgeoisee! . . . This! This!" poured forth the now illumined seer, as he pivoted back again to face the morass of faces beyond the footlights in the murk of that enormous room—"This is Revelation through the medium and convention of form, of colour, of idea. . . ."

"Ah! Yus! . . ." gasped Verecundia from the front row. She recognized the phrase.

"This is what the Divine in Man—or Man in the Divine—or what is both Human and Divine in Divine Humanity or Human Divinity"—he was halting with emotion—"This is what, by one brush wielded in one hand unique, could be interpreted to mankind."

Vavassour paused, only just long enough to strike a final pose. With his right arm as stiff as a sign-post pointing it outward, starboard to the Masterpiece, his right arm lifted vaguely, he completed the message, "Here, alone, is Bourrot!"

"NONSENSE!"

A raucous voice bearing thick traces of a once Oxford accent acquired at Fareham College in Queen Victoria's reign tore the dark air. It came from right at the back near the door, and was in sound and discord like a hip-bath falling downstairs in the midst of a quartet of violins.

"I protest! It's a fraud! No, I will *not* be silenced. . . . This daub. . . ."

Heads turned in the darkness. The Duke, immeasurably relieved, barked "'Ear! 'Ear!" Old Lord Gunter croaked "What's that?" and coughed damnably.

The voice rose, excited to frenzy.

"With all the power at my command I protest against this falsehood! It's no more a Bourrot than I'm a . . ."

But he got no farther! Verecundia, with the decision which (plus twenty millions) had made her, was on her feet and groping for the main switch behind the nearest velvet.

She turned it on, and the flooding light revealed, struggling violently by the doorway, swaying in the grasp of two strong young men and shouting, "I will not be silenced!" the formidable figure of Dr. Mowlen.

"I will not be silenced!" roared the large mouth in the large head, as the two squat arms wrestled fiercely in the grip of his captors.

"The picture's a forgery! The original. . . ."

"Shut up!" squealed Ardee.

". . . is in the possession. . . ."

"Stuff his mouth, Billy! . . ." came smartly from Verecundia herself, a Cæsaress in the crisis of battle. But Billy was slow at orders, and before he could cram his big silk handkerchief into the Professorial gullet the fatal words had issued.

". . . possession of the Duque de Emonsillado y Manuada y wa—Ow! wa—wough—wough. Ouf! Crwk—Crwk—G-ff-ff . . ." and now he was effectually stifled, but the name of the Duke and his copy had gone abroad irrecoverably.

"Who?" asked one. "Oh, the man in the trial.

Other voices said fifty things in different ways. "That bounder?" cried Horse. "Well, what's his manners got to do with it," said Peach, "if he's got the real picture?" And Pig Hamilton was chanting: "Oh! I know! The Rastaquouère!" and Ganzer was mildly repeating, "So? Who? The Duke of St. Ives also?"

"Duke of *what?*" said the Royalty, on its feet amid the hubbub.

"Aw! Duke o' Nothing!" howled the agonized Verecundia, forgetting all etiquette. "Annything . . . Never mind! . . ." Her hands were clasped and she was oblivious to all but the dreadful crisis.

"Turf him out, Billy!" she sang above the mob. "Get a cab! Noh! Plunge him into Jenny's car. Call the police! Tie him up! . . . Oh!" (collapsing on to her chair) "Ah don't know what Ah'm saying!"

Archibald Dacy sprang to her side.

"Let me deal with him!" he hissed grimly. He'd only come off best in one fight in all his life, but the recent memory of it filled his aged heart with courage. "Let me deal with the fellow!" And he forged his way through the press, gnashing his false teeth, to where the unfortunate Counter-Expert of the Imperial Museum was being hustled and hurried into the awaiting car. After all it was fairly safe, the old fool was in strong hands; but it would be fun to kick him as he was shoved through the door. It would soothe his barked shin. So went Archibald forward with bright anger in his heart, and about him that seething torrent of the rich and their parasites swirled and eddied towards the door.

As for Vavassour, he had slipped back into the little side room off the stage, after cleverly switching off the footlights: there he munched sandwiches and drank champagne to his delight. In the main space of the ballroom, where all were straining their necks to see what passed at the door or (the more eager) to take part in the chase and capture, two alone lingered behind near the stage, with wider and wider belts of empty chairs between them, the ebbing tide of super-taxables. They were the twin connoisseurs, Monsieur Caen and Signor Alessandria.

Profiting by a moment when Monsieur Caen was peering with too much caution at the lessening crowd, to make sure his opportunity had come, Signor Alessandria, with Italian, or rather Maltese, agility, leapt on to the stage and slithered to the Masterpiece. He would see that Cross and learn its colour. Not a second later Monsieur Caen had satisfied himself that all was clear, and with Gallic acrobatics had bounded to the same goal—he would see that circle! Each peered behind the canvas at the same moment. Each made the Great Discovery. There was no Rough Circle, no Cross—green, blue, yellow, black, or Femme Enragée. There was nothing. Henry Bensington had proved their master.

Their eyes met behind that famous canvas in that one snatched instant of exploration, and two soft words

Simultaneous curiosity of two great continental experts in modern art

were exchanged. "Ach! Der Lügner!" murmured Monsieur Caen. "Was für ein Genie!" murmured Signor Alessandria.

With the rapidity of the lesser felines each slipped back to the platform-edge, leapt from it silently to the thickly-carpeted floor, and joined the tail of the issuing throng. All faces were turned towards the door. None had espied their curiosity.

* * * * *

EPILOGUE

In the depths of the Plantagenet Hotel the Duke of Emonsillado meditated. Things had not gone as he had expected.

If the case had gone against him there would have been nothing more to be said—or done. If it had gone against Verecundia everything would be over and exactly as he had wanted it to be. But as things were, it was a muddle and it left a ragged edge.

The Duke of Emonsillado was annoyed. Verecundia could trust to time and to her presence in London and to her power as a hostess. In a few years everybody in England would be taking for granted that her copy was the right one. Some few might drop a phrase less and less often about a disputed picture in the South of France. But what good was that?

Then once more, and I hope not for the last time, there came into this man's life inspiration.

You may have noticed, graceful reader, that Fortune never does things by halves. If she gives a man a vast revenue, an ancient title, a strong constitution, and the invaluable absence of conscience, honour and all irritants, she will do other things for him as well. And that is very kind of her. So she inspired the Duke of

Emonsillado. She told him that, though Verecundia might make good with time, for the moment Dr. Mowlem's inrush had put her in agony. This (prompted Fortune) was the Duke's opportunity. He smiled the grim smile which foreran his triumphs, went downstairs, drove straight to Norbolt House, sent in his name to Verecundia, trusted to the *Attaque brusquée* (I don't know the German for it), and succeeded. She received him. She was white with passion, but she received him.

He coolly sat down, though she remained standing for half a minute after. He didn't speak till she had sat down too.

"See here, Vurry," he said. "Ah've come to think all this quarrel's foolishness."

"Yeh do?" was the choked reply.

"Yus, Ah do. Ah was thinkin' las' night how all these years to come you'll be itchin' jus' 'cos Ah've got it—that Other One"—and he wagged his head sideways. "Doan' seem fair, doan' seem right."

Verecundia began to marvel. What was this new mood in her vile enemy, the viler enemy for that he had been childhood's friend?

The Duke crossed his legs, leaned back in his chair, and looked up at the ceiling.

"There ye'll be, Vurry, never sot and fixed, allus itchin'. Aw! Ah'll let yer 'ave it back!"

"You . . ." began the astonished Verecundia, half rising. The Duke still contemplated Heaven.

"Yus. Ah'll let yer 'ave it back—at jest cost price. Ah wouldn't make a cowrie out of ye."

"Cost price," came from Verecundia.

"Twenty thousand," came from the Duke, his head still well back and his eyes still on the ceiling.

"Why, Hardham Emonsillado . . ." began Verecundia. "Aint yeh 'shamed o' yehself ? '"

"Naw!" said the Duke. "It's clean fair. I doan' make a bean out 'o ye. And see here, Vurry, you're sot fer life. No more fantags, no more itch. There just won't be any other Masterpiece, only your Masterpiece!" He sat up straight again and looked at his watch. "Wow!" he said.

"When . . ." began Vurry. She saw the future very clearly indeed before her eyes, and the immense advantage.

The Duke spoke again.

"Ah brought it with me. It's in the hall now."

They sent for it.

The Duke looked at his watch once more.

"Ah'm goin' now, Vurry. Ah've got a date."

"Doan' go, Hardy," said the Fifteenth Marchioness with something tender in her tone, which women know how to assume.

"Vurry well, Vurry."

She sat down at the table, pen in hand and cheque book before her. He stood up at her side. She was making out the cheque in her large, decided hand: twenty thousand pounds; she handed it to him. For

Capitulation of Verecundia, Fifteenth Marchioness of Norbolt, Twenty-first Countess of Pulborough, Thirty-third Baroness Workup in the County of Northumberland, to Hardham, Duque de Emonsillado y Palomar y Manuada y Bo

a moment she was afraid he might offer to kiss her—after all these years. But there was nothing doing. He went out—not as quickly as courtesy permitted, but quicker. Now there was only One Masterpiece in the world. Or rather, there were Three, but the Three were One. *Omne Trinum.* And Verecundia held all of It or Them, and was at rest.

FINIS

SUPER-EPILOGUE

I ALWAYS like my books to have a happy ending. And in case you should miss it, I will point it out as I have done before in other books. Everybody is happy at the end of this book. Verecundia is happy because, though she has paid twenty thousand pounds three times over, it is no more to her than twenty thousand pence, and she has got the Masterpiece(s), and there is no rival. The Duke is happy because he has got out of an *impasse*—twenty thousand up. Mr. Gabriel is happy because he has got five hundred pounds. Henry Bensington is very, very happy, because he has got plenty of money, a good digestion, and does everybody all round. The Young Artist is happy, the Temporary Odd Man is happy, Caen and Alessandria are fairly happy (at not having gone to jail); Ardee will be happy, and so will Elless, because Darling Verecundia is going to give each of them a nice little present. The Dowager is happy, because she has heard some still more abominable scandal. Even poor old Goatcher is happy, for, after all, he found the picture, didn't he?

By the way, the policeman who watched the Duke

so suspiciously in Chelsea is happy. He was warmly commended when they found out who the Duke was for not having done anything silly, and is now trusted on the most delicate work in the Parks.

FAREWELL !

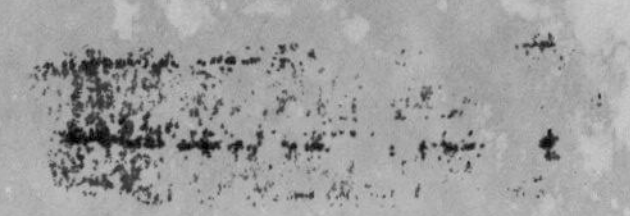